GIFT
HORSE

BETTY LEVIN

GIFT HORSE

Illustrated by Jos. A. Smith

A TRUMPET CLUB SPECIAL EDITION

ISBN 0-590-36295-X

Text copyright © 1996 by Betty Levin.
Illustrations copyright © 1996 by Jos. A. Smith.
All rights reserved. Published by Scholastic Inc., 555 Broadway,
New York, NY 10012, by arrangement with Greenwillow Books,
a division of William Morrow & Company, Inc.

TRUMPET and the TRUMPET logo are registered trademarks of Scholastic Inc.

12 11 10 9 8 7 6 5 4 3 2 1   7 8 9/9 0 1 2/0

Printed in the U.S.A.   40

First Scholastic printing, September 1997

FOR MARGARET

1 ⫾ MATT STARED at the imaginary line his older brother, Alan, had just drawn. It looped around the mattress laid out for Matt on the floor across from Alan's bed. Matt would have to cross the line just to get to his side of the room.

Linda watched from the doorway. "Those spaces aren't equal," she said.

Alan shrugged. "Remember," he told Matt, "every time you invade my territory, I take one of your toys."

"Wait till Mom and Dad find out," Linda declared.

"Not to keep," Alan explained. "What would I do with a bunch of plastic horses our little brother should've outgrown years ago? They'll be like hostages. To teach Matt to respect the rules of my room."

Linda said, "You don't have to outgrow everything. The horses I didn't give Matt are still on my shelf."

"So what?" Alan retorted. "It's not like you play with them. Anyway, it's different for you. Horses are a girl thing."

Matt trudged downstairs to his own room. He had heard all this before. It was Linda who had first gotten him hooked on horses. That was before she moved on to gymnastics. No one at school knew anything about his horses and cowboy stuff except Jerry, his best friend from across the street.

Mom was clearing out the bureau and Dad was tossing toys into a carton.

"Want any of this in Alan's room?" Dad asked.

Matt shook his head. The less that was there, the less Alan could take away from him. "How long is Uncle Oliver staying?" Matt asked.

Mom shoved an emptied drawer back into the bureau. "He didn't say."

"He never does," Dad remarked. "He never asks if it's convenient either. Every few years he just appears."

Mom frowned at Dad. "Don't be so hard on Oliver. He has no way of knowing what we're up to these days. Last time he came I wasn't even working full-time."

"Still, you had your hands full. Not that he'd notice."

"Well, it was fine. Remember, you'd taken Matt out to visit your parents. So there was plenty of room. And Alan and Linda heard all about his adventures."

"What kind of adventures?" Matt asked.

"Oh, meeting the Abominable Snowman in darkest Tibet," declared Dad.

"Gene!" Mom exclaimed, as if Dad had just said something bad.

"Cool," said Matt. "The one that no one's seen except his giant footprints?"

"Your father's teasing," Mom said, staring hard at Dad. Then she added, "You know Uncle Oliver makes films about rare animals. That's why he gets to climb mountains in remote places."

Matt wondered how a mountain climber would fit into this room, which was the smallest in the house. Where would he put all his gear, the ropes and everything?

Matt's room was where Uncle Oliver always stayed

because it was just off the front hall, away from most of the family commotion. The time before last Matt had been a baby in a crib. It had been easy to move him out then. Years ago.

"You want to take some of your horses?" Mom asked him.

Thinking of Alan's threat, Matt shook his head. But when his mother held up Midnight, the black horse with the bridle and saddle you could take off and put on, out went Matt's hands. He carried Midnight upstairs, torn between wanting him on the mattress and wanting him hidden somewhere safe.

At the door to Alan's room Matt faltered. "Is it okay if I cross the line just going in and out?"

Looking up from his video game, Alan nodded.

Matt stepped over the invisible line as if it were a real obstacle on the way to the mattress. Once there, though, he felt trapped. The video game sounded like cartoon chases and car crashes. Clutching Midnight, Matt waited for something to happen.

2 | MOM AND DAD made a special dinner for Uncle Oliver. When he didn't show up, Mom figured the plane was late. She said the children could go ahead and eat and then get ready for bed. The grown-ups would hold out awhile longer.

Alan and Linda wanted to wait, too. This was Friday, so it didn't matter if they stayed up late.

Mom looked at Dad, and Dad looked at the clock. So the older kids ate celery and carrot sticks and insisted that would hold them.

Matt longed for a peanut butter and jelly sandwich with a glass of milk, but he didn't want to be treated any differently. Still, he thought, it was different for Alan and Linda. They could remember Uncle Oliver. For them he was worth the wait.

"Why did we go away the last time Uncle Oliver came?" Matt asked his father.

"Let's see," Dad answered. "Wasn't that after Grandpa had been sick? Yes, and I'd taken Alan and Linda once before. Grandma and Grandpa were afraid you'd forget them. So off we went. Remember? Remember the zoo?"

In an instant it came back to Matt. "There was a baby deer. It bumped me."

"A fawn, yes. And while Grandma took your picture, the duckling you were holding messed all over you."

"Did I mind?" Matt knew he'd made a terrible fuss about it. He hoped Dad wouldn't be able to recall that.

But Dad laughed. "You went off like a siren. What a time we had shutting you up."

Mercifully the ringing doorbell put an end to Dad's story. Shoving each other, Alan and Linda raced to answer it. Matt went along with Mom and Dad. He stared up at the tall man with so much white hair it looked like a mane. If Alan told Uncle Oliver that Matt had wailed like a siren when a duck went to the bathroom on him, Matt would explain that it had happened ages ago, when he was only about four or five.

During all the greetings in the front hall Dad kept trying to move everyone into the dining room.

"But I've eaten," Uncle Oliver finally declared. "Didn't I tell you Nigel was meeting me at the airport—?"

"Yes, but—"

"—to get a head start on some planning. We had to talk before I get to the studio. We had a drink at the airport, then went over to the hotel for dinner. Not bad."

The special meal was brought to the table. Matt's brother and sister dug in, but Matt was so sleepy now that his appetite was gone.

While the rest of the family ate, Uncle Oliver brought in packages wrapped in newspaper. Out came treasures. First there was a small, elaborate rug for Mom and Dad. Mom exclaimed over the intricate weaving, the deep colors. Next came a fossil. Mastodon dung, Uncle Oliver told Alan. Poop, Dad translated.

"Isn't that awfully . . . valuable?" asked Mom.

Uncle Oliver shrugged. "I thought Alan would like it."

"Like it!" Alan grinned up at Uncle Oliver. "It's the best."

Linda's present was a polar bear tooth, ragged and hollow at one end, tapered and smooth at the other.

There was one more package. Uncle Oliver hesitated ever so slightly before handing it to Matt. It had to be really special. But what? Something light. An ostrich egg? Matt's best friend's father was planning to hatch an egg from an emu, a bird sort of like an ostrich, so Matt understood how precious an egg like that was. He would make room for it in a safe place on his shelf. No one would be allowed to touch it.

Off came the paper with odd, squiggly print in another language. The thing was not an egg, big or small. It was a soft ball, light as a feather, the sort of toy Matt's best friend's baby sister might have in her playpen.

"Oh, how pretty!" exclaimed Mom when Matt forgot to say thank you.

"What is it?" asked Alan.

"A ball," said Uncle Oliver unnecessarily. "I'm afraid," he added, "I got stuck in a time warp. The last time I saw you, Matt, you were so little."

"You mean it's a baby toy?" Alan snorted.

"It's much more than that," Mom insisted, rushing in to bolster the gift or Matt or Uncle Oliver. "See, that's such soft leather, and with lovely tooling."

"It's okay," sleepy Matt managed to mumble to Uncle Oliver. "An ostrich egg might've come cracked." He staggered off to bed, not even bothering to step over the imaginary line. Groping for Midnight, he nudged the soft baby ball down to the foot of the mattress and made room on his pillow for the hard plastic horse.

3] THE HOUSE WAS so quiet that Matt figured everyone was still asleep. Sitting up, he looked across at Alan all bunched up under the covers. There on the bureau beside the bed was the lump of mastodon dung. Matt padded over to it.

"Don't touch," came Alan's voice from beneath the bedclothes.

"I wasn't going to," Matt answered. Alan must have X-ray vision. "I didn't get a good look at it last night."

Alan rolled over and pulled the sheet off his face. He didn't speak, but Matt could feel Alan's eyes sweeping down to the floor. Matt had crossed the line. He froze, waiting for Alan to demand the horse.

The longer Matt stood as if rooted to the floor, the longer the silence stretched between them. Then it came to Matt that Midnight wasn't his only toy here. There was that ball thing Uncle Oliver had given him. Matt swung around, dived onto the mattress, grasped his horse in one hand, the ball in the other, tossed the ball onto Alan's bed, and pounded out to the hall.

All he could think of was putting Midnight out of Alan's reach. If only he could get past Uncle Oliver without waking him. Matt thumped downstairs and stopped outside his own door, which was ajar. Maybe he could tiptoe into the room. He shoved the door just enough to glimpse his bed. Empty! What luck! All Matt had to do was run to his shelf and stick Midnight in behind some of the other horses.

Walking in, he stopped in his tracks. There on the floor, surrounded by film boxes, folders, disks, and a laptop computer, sprawled Uncle Oliver, who nodded a welcome and said, "Anyone else up?"

Matt said he didn't think so. He walked to the horse shelf and placed Midnight on his side so that he wouldn't stand out among the others.

Uncle Oliver watched Matt and then asked, "Did you want an ostrich egg?"

Matt looked down at the big man on the floor and said, "I just tried to guess what it was."

Uncle Oliver shook his head. "I only remembered your sister and brother."

Matt nodded. "I know. It's all right."

"Next time—" Uncle Oliver began.

"It's all right," Matt repeated. "I already found something to do with the ball."

Uncle Oliver folded his long legs under him and rose to his great height. "If you could have just one thing, what would it be?"

It was hard to look at Uncle Oliver when he stood so tall, so Matt stared down at the laptop computer.

"Surely not!" exclaimed Uncle Oliver. "Do you really crave this kind of gadget?"

Matt said, "A horse."

"What a relief!" declared Uncle Oliver. "Do you mean a horse like the one you just put away?"

Matt shook his head. "I mean, you know, real."

Uncle Oliver made a sound like Dad with his mouth full of toothpaste. Usually Dad had to spit out the toothpaste before Matt could understand him. But Uncle Oliver only had to swallow a gulp of nothing to make himself clear. "Real. Naturally." He was nodding his shaggy white head. "Well"—Uncle Oliver went on—"and why not?" He seemed to be talking about something he meant to do. Then he added, "I suppose you mean a pony."

"No, a horse. That a cowboy could use or a trick rider in a circus."

"A pony would be easier for you to handle, though," Uncle Oliver pointed out.

Matt stood firm. "A horse. I've always wanted one, even when I was little."

Uncle Oliver gave this some thought. Then he said, "How about a small horse?"

"I guess that would be okay," Matt responded. He could hardly believe that he sounded so calm when inside he felt like whooping with joy.

At this moment Matt's mother poked her head inside the room and told Matt he wasn't supposed to bother Uncle Oliver. But Uncle Oliver assured Mom that they were just reaching an important meeting of minds. After she had gone, Uncle Oliver said to Matt, "You do understand, it's not the sort of thing that can be arranged at a moment's notice. Not if it's to be exactly right."

Matt nodded. "I can wait."

"Good," said Uncle Oliver. "I won't forget. That's a promise."

Matt believed him. Matt loved him. Going back to Alan's room to get dressed, Matt felt like someone who had just climbed the highest mountain peak in darkest somewhere. There before him, waiting to be discovered, stretched a glorious new world.

4 | EVERYONE EXCEPT MATT had things to do, places to go. Before Mom went out, she reminded Matt to stay out of Uncle Oliver's room. Dad asked what harm there was in letting Matt play in his own room while Oliver was at the television station. Mom nodded at the piles of stuff left on the floor. Then she shut the door with a firm click. Dad shrugged at Matt and told him he could go over to Jerry's house, which was like Matt's second home.

The two boys usually went there after school because Jerry's grandmother, Serena, stayed at home with Jerry's little sister while his parents were at work.

"So how's the famous uncle?" Serena asked Matt.

"He's going to get me a horse," Matt told her. "To make up for bringing me a baby toy."

"What kind of baby toy?" Jerry wanted to know. "What did he get the others?"

"A chunk of mastodon dung," said Matt. "And a polar bear tooth."

"Dung?" asked Jerry.

"Poop," Matt informed him.

"I'd rather have a baby toy," Serena remarked.

"It doesn't smell or anything. It's thousands of years old. It's worth a lot."

Serena shook her head. "No accounting," she said. "So what kind of horse are you getting?"

"Not a pony," he said. "Real," he said.

"Cool!" Jerry exclaimed. "We better clean out your garage."

Serena said to him, "Don't go turning things upside down in the Hoffmans' carriage house." Serena always called the barn a carriage house because way back when many of the houses on Plympton Street were built, people kept horses and carriages in the downstairs of their barns and hay up above. Jerry's house had once been a barn like that before it was converted into a people house. But Matt's family lived in one of the original houses and kept the car in the barn beside it.

Matt's dad hoped to turn part of the barn into an office someday when he and Mom went into business for themselves. But right now you couldn't have a business, not even a travel agency, on Plympton Street. So there was no reason not to get one of the stalls ready for Uncle Oliver's gift horse.

The boys went straight to the barn. They couldn't see over all the junk piled up beyond the space for the car. There were dozens of cartons, a broken gym set, a filing cabinet, a bed and several mattresses, bicycle wheels and handlebars, a baby stroller, stacks of plywood full of nail holes, skis, a wading pool, and a steel bookcase loaded with tools, paint cans, and old pots and pans.

Jerry sighed. "It's going to be a big job," he said.

"I don't think the horse is coming for a while," Matt answered. Jerry's enthusiasm confirmed his own belief in Uncle Oliver's promise.

"I guess your dad and mom will help," Jerry said. "Won't they?" he added when Matt didn't reply.

"Probably," Matt finally said. "We haven't had a chance to talk about it yet."

Jerry digested this statement. "They don't know," he declared. "They don't even know you're getting a horse."

Matt said, "Maybe Uncle Oliver told them. I don't know. He was in a hurry this morning. So was Mom."

But a germ of uneasiness had invaded Matt's innermost feelings. "I wonder how much space a horse needs," he said.

"You better ask your uncle," Jerry advised.

Matt shook his head. He didn't dare raise any question about the horse now that he and his uncle had reached that meeting of minds. If it had come about so quickly, couldn't it just as easily fall apart? "I don't know Uncle Oliver all that well," he explained.

Jerry looked surprised. "I know my uncles. All three of them."

"He's not exactly my uncle." Matt went over all the talk that had gone back and forth about Uncle Oliver before he arrived. "He's like Mom's uncle." Now it came to Matt. "He's my great-uncle."

"Well, he's a great uncle, all right," Jerry agreed, "if he promised to send you a horse. My uncles wouldn't do anything that great."

Matt nodded. He felt better again. Trust in Uncle Oliver nudged against the uneasiness that had settled in like a cold coming on. Since the horse couldn't be arranged for at a moment's notice, he guessed he'd better get used to this uneasiness and try to look on the bright side. A good, long wait would give everyone time to get ready for this addition to the Hoffman family.

5 ⫾ JERRY AND HIS father, who came to see the mastodon dung, picked up the Hoffmans' Sunday paper. They were just in time for breakfast.

When Matt's mother introduced them to Uncle Oliver, Jerry explained that his dad was Leroy to everyone except Alan, who had to call him Mr. Brewster because he was in his science class in school.

"Science?" asked Uncle Oliver. "What are kids learning these days?"

That started the kind of conversation kids tune out. Jerry and Matt drifted into the kitchen to look for store-bought jelly because the homemade jam on the table was full of seeds. When the voices in the dining room rose, Matt began to listen to them. And then he listened even harder because Leroy's voice dropped in a way that could mean he didn't want Matt or Jerry to hear. Leroy mentioned wrong impressions, confusion. What was Leroy talking about?

"Clear it up then," Matt's father ordered, sounding slightly annoyed.

Uncle Oliver's low voice rumbled a reply.

"It's got to have something to do with the horse," Matt whispered to Jerry.

"Seriously, Oliver," Matt's mother insisted. "You won't forget?"

"Of course he won't," Matt murmured. "He's promised. Anyway, it's between Uncle Oliver and me."

"You sure your mom's talking about the horse?" Jerry asked.

Matt shrugged. "We're the only ones not in there, and they think we can't hear."

Nodding, Jerry dug the spoon into the grape jelly, realized his toast was gone, and slipped the spoonful into his mouth.

Leroy and Jerry stayed so long that Jerry's mother came over to see what was going on. By now the grown-ups were in the living room, the Sunday paper spread out around their coffee cups. Linda was on the telephone. Alan was in his room with the door closed.

In the dining room Matt and Jerry had all the chairs on their sides to make partitions and fences for a stable. Jerry convinced Matt to get one of his plastic horses off the shelf in Uncle Oliver's room. Matt had to get permission to go in there. Standing at the entrance to the living room, he explained that he needed Midnight to work with. Uncle Oliver nodded and waved him on.

"There," said Jerry's mother. "The boys aren't confused. It's just serious play."

"Not play," Jerry called from the dining room. "Work. We need a model because we're planning."

"Right," said the parents in chorus. "Work."

Returning with Midnight, Matt could tell from their tones that they were exchanging the kinds of smiles that showed how much smarter they were than their kids. He could feel the heat rise in his face. His ears were about to turn red.

Then he and Jerry considered what kind of equipment they would need to take care of a horse in this setup, and he went off to find the pail and brush that were usually left at the top of the cellar stairs.

By the time he got back to the dining room, the grown-ups and their superior smiles were forgotten. Jerry had rearranged the chairs to make a corral, Western style. Matt knew where there was some clothesline that would make a lariat. Leaving Midnight in the corral with a model bale of hay that was really shredded wheat, the boys went outside to practice roping.

6 | UNCLE OLIVER CUT short his stay. Since some of the film he had brought with him turned out to have been damaged, he had to rush back to Baffin Island before winter darkness made filming impossible.

Matt's mother tried to talk him into leading a wildlife tour in that area next year. But he wouldn't consider it.

There was no telling what part of the world he'd be in by then. Besides, he didn't lead tours.

Dad told Mom to let it go. Cruises and trips to Disney World were more to their clients' liking. But Mom raised the subject again after Uncle Oliver had gone. "A wildlife tour might appeal to people looking for something new and exotic."

"And safe and comfortable?" Dad pointed out. "That sort of tour runs to a lot of money. Too much for our clients' pocketbooks."

Thoughtfully Mom peeled an orange. Supper was over, but the family lingered at the table. Then she spoke up again. "How will we know if there's a demand for a wildlife tour if we don't ever offer one?"

"I'd go," Alan declared. "How about a safari?"

"Me, too," said Linda. "Only let's go to an island with palm trees."

Grinning, Dad turned to Matt. "What's your choice? We might as well get all the votes in before we count them."

Everyone started talking at once, as if the tour were already a real possibility, only the location up for grabs. No one heard Matt try to explain that he couldn't think about going anywhere until he could figure out who would take care of his horse. "Maybe Jerry," he suggested, and Alan, hearing only the name, said, "It'll be too expensive to take someone else's kid."

Mom's voice rose above the others. "It's not happening. Dad was teasing."

Alan shoved his chair back. "Then I'm out of here," he declared.

"Don't go too far," Mom told him. "It's your night to clear the table."

Matt asked how far away was the place where Uncle Oliver had gone.

"You mean Baffin Island? It's up north in Canada."

Matt tried to imagine Uncle Oliver finding a horse up north in Canada. "Is he coming back here afterward?" Matt asked.

Dad said, "He's not likely to grace us with another personal appearance as long as we're prepared. He likes to wait till it's inconvenient."

"Really, Gene," Mom objected. "You're too hard on Oliver. Did it ever occur to you that he might get lonely for family? We're all he has."

"Is he poor?" Matt asked, suddenly worried about whether Uncle Oliver had enough money to pay for the horse.

"Ha!" said Dad, which meant "not hardly."

Matt heaved a sigh of relief. Uncle Oliver had warned

Matt that it might take awhile to get a horse. Probably he'd tend to it on his way to his next adventure. Meanwhile there was plenty to do to get ready. "When can me and Jerry get started clearing out a stall?" Matt wanted to know.

"Jerry and I," Dad told him.

"You'll do it, too?" Matt exclaimed. "Cool. There's a lot of heavy stuff in the way."

"Did I miss something?" Mom asked. "What're you talking about?"

"The stall." Matt stood up as tall as he could to make his point. "We'll need a place for him."

"For Uncle Oliver?" Alarm spread across Dad's face. "Oliver's moving into our future office space? I think I'm having a nightmare."

"Gene!" Mom exclaimed. "Give Matt a chance to tell us why he thinks he needs a stall. No," she added, beckoning Matt closer, "I'm beginning to guess why. Oliver forgot to have that talk with you, didn't he?"

Matt was filled with confusion. Of course Uncle Oliver had spoken with him. They had reached a meeting of minds. "No," said Matt. "I mean, yes. We talked."

"What did he say?" Mom demanded.

Alan, his hands full of stacked plates, paused to hear Matt's reply.

Matt made a stab at a right answer. "That it might take awhile?"

Mom looked from Matt to Dad. Dad just shrugged. "Your uncle," he reminded her.

"Great-uncle," Matt corrected.

Alan nodded. "He's Mom's uncle, our great-uncle, and he's not sending you a horse."

"You don't know!" Matt retorted.

"Right," declared Alan with a snicker. "And I'm getting an elephant."

Matt thrust out his chin and stood his ground. No one, not even Alan, had any idea what had happened that morning in Uncle Oliver's room.

Mom was speaking now. "What we're trying to tell you, Matt, is that Uncle Oliver likes to . . . He wanted to make you happy."

Matt nodded. "I know. He did."

"Nice going," Dad murmured to Mom. "Let me know when it's my turn."

Mom swung around, caught sight of Alan balancing the plates, and waved him on to the kitchen. She followed to make sure they made it safely to the counter.

"So." Dad leaned back in a friendly way. "So what do you suppose Uncle Oliver has in mind? Practically speaking."

Matt guessed this was a sort of test. Suddenly bed seemed like a good idea.

"I mean," prompted Dad, lowering his voice, "I guess you're looking forward to this horse."

Matt nodded. If Dad kept on talking, then Matt wouldn't have to say anything.

Dad thought a moment. He cleared his throat. "Funny thing about certain grown-ups," he said. "They may promise something they can't deliver. See, Uncle Oliver would like to make good on his promise, but he's probably put it out of his mind by now. He wouldn't realize that you're counting on the horse to show up sometime soon."

"I'm not," Matt responded. "Uncle Oliver already told me that. I just want to fix up the stall."

"Oh, well, good." Dad nodded vigorously. "Why not? As long as you understand. We'd hate to have you waiting, hoping—"

"I understand," Matt almost shouted. Why did Dad need so much reassuring? What was the matter with him and Mom?

Then and there Matt decided to keep his thoughts to himself from now on, at least where the actual horse was concerned.

Leaving for his room, Matt heard Dad call to Mom

that there didn't seem to be a problem after all. Matt was fine, Dad told her as he brushed crumbs from the table into his hand. It couldn't do any harm to let Matt and Jerry take their serious horse play out to the barn. There was nothing to worry about.

7 | THANKSGIVING CAME AND went. So did Christmas, with not so much as a card from Uncle Oliver. Matt decided that Uncle Oliver hadn't forgotten his promise; he was simply too far from civilization.

Meanwhile progress on the stall lurched forward in fits and starts. Matt's father, who had actually helped Matt and Jerry get started, lost interest in the project once the things blocking the way to the stall got moved into his car space and blocked the car. "Someday," he told Matt, "we'll make a clean sweep of everything, and your mother and I will hang out our shingle." Matt wasn't sure what Dad meant by this, except that it signaled an end to his help.

Then Jerry's father got involved because Serena, who was his mother, threatened to throw out his bats. Normally Jerry's father kept the bats in a small refrigerator in his science room at school. They could hibernate quite comfortably in a refrigerator that kept an even, cool temperature. But he brought them home over Christmas vacation in case the power was cut off during repair work in school.

But when Serena saw them in her family's refrigerator hanging upside down from the top rack next to the egg box and tomorrow's casserole, she had a fit. "Leroy Brewster," she declared, "are you going through a second childhood or what?"

"It's just for a couple of weeks, Ma," Jerry's father said.

"That's what you used to say about tadpoles in the bathroom sink."

"Do we have tadpoles?" Jerry exclaimed. "I thought they only happened in the spring."

"You're right about tadpoles," Leroy told Jerry. "Your grandmother's dredging up old complaints, that's all."

Matt soaked up every word. Brewster family arguments were much more interesting than his own family's. Besides, there was nothing in his refrigerator to rival those small brown creatures all lined up, their leathery wings folded close to their velvet bodies.

"Don't keep opening the refrigerator door," Serena told Matt and Jerry, who hoped that if they stood there long enough, at least one bat would show some sign of life. "You'll refrigerate the whole house."

"Yes, keep that door closed," Jerry's father added, "or the warm air from the kitchen will wake up the bats." A warning that only drew the boys more and more often to the Brewsters' refrigerator.

In the end it was Jerry's mother who sealed the bats' fate. She made a big batch of eggnog for the Brewsters' New Year's Eve open house and set the punch bowl in the bottom of the refrigerator. When the lukewarm eggnog raised the temperature inside the refrigerator, some of the bats began to wake up. Sleepily they relaxed their grip, only to drop into the bowl below and drown in the thick, frothy liquid.

Matt, who was helping his mother carry dips and cheese over to the Brewsters', arrived in time to hear Jerry's father shout, "My bats!"

Jerry's mother, running into the kitchen to see what all the fuss was about, shrieked, "My eggnog!"

"Out of here," Matt's mother commanded, herding Jerry as well as Matt to the front door. "You'd better come over," she told Jerry. "They've got enough on their hands."

"But I can help," Jerry protested.

"So can I," Matt chimed in. "What are they going to do with the bats?"

"I don't know," Mom replied. "I don't want to know."

"I do," Matt insisted.

But Mom kept Jerry and Matt in the Hoffman house until it was so late that they didn't even want to go back, especially if they had to get dressed in good clothes because of the company. And when they woke up the next morning in Matt's room, it was a whole new year later.

They went to the barn to work on the stall and found a long extension cord and a small refrigerator there. Matt and Jerry allowed themselves one quick glimpse inside. The four remaining bats looked just the same as always. By the time Jerry's father showed up to check on these survivors, the boys were using the hayrack in the corner for a basket and seeing how far back they could stand to shoot Uncle Oliver's baby ball into it.

"Look at this wonderful space!" Jerry's father exclaimed. And before they knew it, he was clearing away more junk from the back of the barn and revealing wonders long concealed.

8 | THE BEST THING Jerry's father uncovered was a trapdoor in the floor in front of the stall. It was nailed shut, but that didn't stop Leroy. He led the two boys outside and around to the back, where there was a sort of shed underneath the barn like an open basement. But garden stuff and stacked wood took up most of the shed. There was no way to get right below the trapdoor. Jerry's father said he would come back later with a crowbar.

Jerry went home with him, and Matt went into his own house. By now everyone was up. He told them about the trapdoor.

"What's it for?" Linda asked.

"Probably it's where they dumped the bedding, the manure," Dad said. "Must have made an awful stink down there. They'd have to back a cart in underneath to haul the stuff away. Maybe someone came around once a week the way the trash truck comes now."

"Why not just let it dry out and turn into a fossil?" asked Matt. "Then it wouldn't smell."

Alan laughed, but Linda explained that it took thousands of years for things like mastodon poop to become fossilized, so it was probably the same with horse manure. Then she added, "But what if the trapdoor wasn't for cleaning out the stalls? There could be a secret passage under the barn. Maybe for hiding runaway slaves."

"Serena will know," Matt said. "Her great-grandfather was a slave. He escaped, and then he helped lots of others escape. There might be a secret passage under the street."

"Good idea," Matt's mother told him. "But the Brewsters only moved to Plympton Street the year after we did."

When Leroy showed up with a heavy, clawed bar, they all bundled up and went out to the barn together.

Mom was afraid an open trapdoor might be dangerous. After all, this was where Matt and Jerry played when it wasn't too cold out.

Not play, Matt felt like yelling. But he knew that if he mentioned Uncle Oliver's horse, Alan would make fun of him and Mom and Dad would explain yet again that Uncle Oliver didn't exactly mean that he would actually send one.

By now the grown-ups had decided they should pry open the trapdoor and then show the kids how to close it flush to the barn floor. Both fathers talked about what could be done with all the newly cleared space. Matt's dad said it would be years before he and Mom would

be able to plan an office here. Jerry's dad said that meanwhile he could put the stall to use for short-term projects.

"Dad'll have to move out when your horse comes," Jerry whispered to Matt.

They retreated to Matt's room. They had just seen a circus special on TV, so they turned the corral into a circus ring and decked out Midnight and a few other horses from Matt's collection in Christmas wrapping paper. Then they went across to Jerry's house for other animals to put in their circus. "What about the drowned bats?" Matt suggested. "We can strap them to the backs of the circus horses."

"They could be flying trapeze animals," Jerry said. "They've got wings."

They started to hunt for the unfortunate creatures, but Serena caught on and put a stop to their search.

"Can we have some of the party food?" Jerry asked, banking on a yes following a no.

Serena let them rummage around for leftover snacks from last night's open house. They tasted exotic dips and stuffed themselves with bite-size cream puffs, but the refrigerator had lost its appeal now that the bats were gone.

9 | JERRY'S FATHER SPENT the next couple of weekends clearing the back of the barn. He lubricated rings bolted into studs in the stall. Now they could be flipped up to feed rope through. He uncovered various lengths of chain, rusted but full of possibility. And around behind an adjoining stall, still crammed with junk, he opened up a corridor lined with harness racks and shelves.

Matt and Jerry helped lug and stack debris. Probably each family that had lived in Matt's house had added to it, at first shoving back out of sight what no one could bear to part with, and then losing interest because of the bird droppings and mouse dirt and dust.

When it got too cold to work without gloves, Jerry's father quit. So Matt and Jerry finally had the place to themselves again. They dug around in dark corners, unearthing horseshoes, leather with buckles, and other objects they didn't recognize. With all these finds now stacked inside the cleared stall, Matt began to understand how easily things could pile up.

When they showed Serena their best horseshoe, she told them horseshoes brought good luck. You had to nail them on the wall with the open end facing up so that the luck wouldn't fall out.

Matt hunted for nails that would fit through the holes in the shoe. He and Jerry dragged a stepladder over to the stall, but they couldn't get it to open. So they tilted the closed ladder up against the stall. Jerry had to lean against it to keep it from sliding while Matt climbed. It was only when he had gone as high as he could that they realized that neither of them could reach the shoe and nails and hammer.

Matt finally managed to scramble onto the top of the stall door, which he straddled while Jerry set the ladder aside and kicked away something to make room for it. The boys heard the familiar sound of lumpy objects settling. Then Jerry handed up the horseshoe, nails, and hammer.

But there were three things for two hands. Two frozen hands. Matt had pulled his mittens off with his teeth. His fingers gripping the horseshoe ached with cold. He seemed to be hugging the doorpost, but he was really holding on for dear life.

The moment he held up the shoe with its nails and then tried to hammer a nail into the wood, he lost his balance. Shoe and nails dropped from his grasp.

Jerry looked for the nails and then went to find more. This time he handed the shoe up to Matt with one nail already set in place. Matt pressed it against the doorpost

and hit as hard as he could. As soon as he dared, he let go of the shoe. It stayed put. Now he could hold the hammer properly and give the nail a good solid whack.

"You got it!" Jerry declared from below.

Matt nodded happily and let the hammer drop. "Ladder," he said through the mittens in his mouth.

"What?"

"Ladder," Matt repeated, spitting out the mittens. He tried to stick his frozen hands inside his jacket, but he needed one hand to hold on.

"It's stuck," Jerry finally told him. Something else had moved when Jerry had shoved the ladder out of the way. He couldn't pull it free.

Matt told him to hurry and get Linda.

But it was Alan who came to the rescue. "What are you doing up there?" he demanded.

Jerry showed him the horseshoe. He showed him the ladder, which Alan tried to drag from beneath a tub that had shifted and was itself pinned down by planks lying across it.

"Just swing your leg over and slide down," Alan told Matt. "I'll grab you."

Matt's hands were so cold that he could barely hold on with them. He swiveled on his stomach, kicked his feet in search of contact until Alan yelled at him to cut it out. Matt let go, clawing the stall door as he slid. Alan caught him, slowing the fall but going down with him. For a moment they lay entangled. Then Alan detached himself and stood up. "You all right?" he asked.

Matt nodded, but his teeth were chattering.

"All for a horseshoe," Alan exclaimed.

"It's for—" Jerry began.

Matt cut in, afraid Jerry would mention Uncle Oliver's horse. "For good luck," Matt explained. "Like it's a clubhouse."

"Good luck! You believe that?" Alan asked.

"You'll see," Jerry blurted. "You'll see when the horse comes and it's exactly what Matt asked for."

Alan laughed. "Dream on," he said. Then he shook his head. "But if it keeps you out of my face, go for it."

He strode away, only to turn back. A friend of his was coming over, he said. Maybe Matt should go to Jerry's house to warm up.

Matt understood that Alan didn't want his friends to see his kid brother playing with toy horses and counting on horseshoes for good luck.

10 | MATT NEEDED TO find out what special days were coming up that Uncle Oliver might know about.

Serena said, "January and February are full of important birthdays."

"Whose?" asked Matt. "Besides Alan's," he added.

Serena picked up Jerry's baby sister and wiped off her face. Missy, who had a cold, didn't know how to blow her nose. Jerry and Matt had tried off and on all afternoon to teach her how, but she just blew milky bubbles back at them and dribbled on. Matt couldn't understand how Serena, who handled all that mess, could have made such a fuss over a few clean bats in the refrigerator. Well, clean until they got eggnog all over them.

When Serena was finished with Missy, she said, "First there's Martin Luther King, Junior. We've already had his birthday. Then come Lincoln and Washington."

Matt remembered about all three of those. Wasn't there anyone else?

"How old are they?" asked Jerry.

"They're dead," Serena told him, which wasn't exactly an answer.

"So no presents," Matt said.

"Right. You know we celebrate their birthdays because they were great men."

"Alan won't get his present either," Matt said. "Ice skates. He got them ahead of time. And a hockey stick."

"That was sensible," Serena said. "The skates wouldn't do him much good when the ice melts."

After Matt's parents got home that night, he probed more deeply into the question of presents. "Do Grandma and Grampa know about Alan's birthday?"

"Of course," they both answered.

"Will they send him a present?"

"Probably just a token," Dad said as he shook the salad bowl to make the greens settle. "Every birthday they put aside some money to help him go to college. They do that for each of you."

"My birthday's in August," Matt told them.

"We know," they said.

Dad squeezed past Mom and washed off more lettuce. "What's on your mind, Matt?" he asked as he shook the leaves over the sink.

Matt couldn't come right out and say "presents." Dad would think he was being greedy. He couldn't mention Uncle Oliver either, or both Mom and Dad would jump to the conclusion that he still expected a horse.

He thought hard. Valentine's Day was all about cards and candy and flowers, so that didn't count. "Nothing," he finally answered, and then suddenly he remembered Easter. But by that time Mom and Dad were talking about something else. Matt picked a carrot slice out of the salad bowl and went to find Linda.

She was on the telephone. Matt settled down for a long wait. He munched the carrot slowly to make it last. Linda lowered her voice and covered the mouthpiece with her hand.

Later Matt asked her what she had given him for Easter last year.

"Nothing," she answered. "We get Easter baskets. I might be too old for one this year."

Matt gave up. There was no gift-giving day in the offing, at least not one likely to attract Uncle Oliver's attention. "It'll be a surprise," he informed Jerry. "Any day now. Be on the lookout for a big truck."

For the next few afternoons the boys kept watch. Since most of Marbury's heavy traffic kept to the business side of town, they could hear any noisy vehicle that came along Common Street and slowed at the end of Plympton. But the only trucks that turned in were delivering mail or express packages somewhere else.

Then, out of the blue, there came with the regular mail a heavy envelope that had been used so often there was almost no room on it for the Hoffmans' address.

"It's from Uncle Oliver," Linda said as she sorted through the rest of the letters.

"Open it," said Matt, his heart pounding.

"It's for Mom," Linda told him.

"We should call her," Matt said. "If he's coming, she'll need to know."

So Linda called the travel agency where Mom and Dad worked. Mom was out, but Dad told Linda that whatever was in the envelope could wait until tonight.

It could wait, thought Matt, but he couldn't. Twice he went to examine the envelope as if its outside could reveal what was inside.

When finally Mom got home and and opened it, even Alan hung around to learn what Uncle Oliver had written. There was a list of dates and addresses where Uncle Oliver could be reached. And there was a brief scribbled note explaining that the list wouldn't do much good since mostly he'd be out of reach in Tasmania.

"Where's Tasmania?" Alan asked.

"Australia," Dad told him.

"I thought he was up north in Canada," Matt said.

"He was," Mom told him, showing the note to Dad, "but now he's doing something else."

"Australia's far away, isn't it?" Matt said, his heart sinking. How could Uncle Oliver arrange for the horse from such a distance?

"Very far," Dad answered. "Well," he went on, "I've heard of wild-goose chases, but this beats them all."

"Uncle Oliver's chasing geese?" Matt said.

"He's joined an expedition," Mom said. "To look for an extinct animal that might not be extinct after all."

"Like a dinosaur?"

"It's called a Tasmanian tiger," Mom said, scanning the letter for more information. "Uncle Oliver's the only outsider who's been invited to join the search. He doesn't know how long it will take." Mom folded the note and stuck it back inside the envelope along with the list of dates and addresses.

"Is that all?" Matt asked her. "Didn't he say anything else?"

Mom shook her head. "Only that some equipment he won't need in Tasmania is being shipped here. We can store it in the barn."

"Typical Oliver," Dad muttered. "Not 'May I, please?' but 'By the way, take care of my stuff.'"

"At least there's room now," Mom pointed out. "Anyway, it might not get here for ages. You know Oliver and his arrangements. It could arrive by packhorse."

With those words, Mom revived all of Matt's hope, which had begun to dim. He and Jerry had been on the lookout for the wrong kind of delivery. It would be just like Uncle Oliver to arrange for his stuff and Matt's horse to be sent together. After all, Uncle Oliver was the kind of person who never threw anything away if it could possibly be used again. That was why he wrapped his small presents in newspaper and recycled old envelopes.

11 | WINTER HUNG ON so long Matt began to imagine that instead of a packhorse delivery Uncle Oliver's stuff would arrive on a horse-drawn sleigh. He imagined a red harness with bells. The harnessed horse would be for him. In his mind's eye the snow was always smooth and white. But outdoors it got grayer and lumpier with every thaw and freeze-up.

Jerry's father revisited the Hoffmans' barn. It was getting closer to the time when he might be getting an emu egg to hatch out.

"Your uncle Oliver better hurry with the horse," Jerry warned Matt. "My dad thinks the stall's for his emu."

"He doesn't need a whole horse stall for a bird," Matt said, but he couldn't help feeling nervous every time he heard Jerry's father talking about the emus and other unusual animals at Wilmot Place.

One Saturday he took Jerry and Matt with him to

Wilmot Place at a special time when it wasn't open to the public. Behind the big, fancy house that was almost a museum there was a kind of park and zoo. The last Mr. Wilmot had collected animals that were endangered or rare. When he died, he left money to keep them there so that all the people of Marbury could see them and learn to protect threatened species.

While Leroy talked with the person in charge of the animals, whose name was Marianne, the boys looked through wire at a pair of emus. Matt wondered why anyone would want such a top-heavy–looking bird. He was drawn to another enclosure where great-eyed furry creatures reclined on tree branches.

"Lemurs," said Marianne.

They were so still he almost asked Marianne if they were stuffed. But she started to tell him about lemurs, which were related to monkeys and came from Madagascar, and he was spared having her find out how dumb he was. Instead he told her about Uncle Oliver's search for a Tasmanian tiger.

"No kidding!" Marianne exclaimed. "Heavy-duty! Was there a sighting?"

Since Matt couldn't answer, Jerry's father and Marianne discussed the chances of finding one (slim) and the challenge (tremendous).

Jerry asked if the tiger was dangerous and whether it would have to be shot.

Marianne explained that it wasn't really a tiger, although it did have stripes. "It's a sort of marsupial wolf," she went on. "Anyway, it looks more like a wolf than a tiger, and the female carries its young in a pouch. What a find that would be!" she declared.

"If emus aren't endangered," Jerry asked as his father drove out between the imposing gateposts, "why are they kept at Wilmot Place?"

"Because they were here before," Leroy replied. "But Mr. Wilmot also provided for some additions. In case other animals became rare or endangered after his time."

Like a Tasmanian tiger, thought Matt. Or wolf. If you were stalking one, how would you know whether to listen for a howl or a roar?

That night Matt's parents announced that next week they were going to a convention together. Serena had agreed to sleep over in the Hoffman house.

Alan said, "Why not just have Matt stay with Jerry? Linda and I don't need someone here."

"It's all arranged," Dad told him. "Serena will do supper, too."

"But we know how to—" Linda protested.

"It's arranged," Dad repeated. And that was that.

After Mom and Dad left on Wednesday, nothing was

really different about the weekday setup. Only it felt weird knowing that they both were far away.

Saturday morning Jerry came to Matt's house before anyone else was up. Since Matt's room was so close to the front door, Jerry had no trouble waking him.

Jerry reported that Missy had roused the Brewster household at the crack of dawn. Everything had gone wrong because Serena was here at the Hoffmans'.

"Can't your mother take care of Missy?" Matt asked.

"It's the only time she gets to sleep late," Jerry explained. "Do you have anything good in your kitchen?"

The boys went to forage for leftovers. They shared a chicken leg and then each took a cupcake and a glass of milk to Matt's room without waking anyone else.

Which is why they were the only ones to hear the truck and trailer pull up in front of the house. Matt had to finish dressing in a hurry. By the time the driver walked up to the front door, the boys were already there, pulling it open, speechless with excitement.

"Looking for Matthew Hoffman," said the driver.

Matt nodded.

"Where's your father?" the driver asked.

Jerry spoke up. "They're away. This is Matthew Hoffman."

The driver looked at Matt. "You expecting a horse?"

Matt nodded.

"Listen, kid, I've been driving all night, and I've got another stop to make, so if you want to stand there not talking, fine, just so's I can get going." He held out a sheaf of papers and a pen. "Sign here, and I'll unload and be on my way." He turned back to Jerry. "Can he do that? Can he sign his name?"

"I better get my father," Jerry said.

But Matt had taken the pen and was writing his name with great care in a box that said: "RECEIVED: HORSE."

Jerry raced off to his house, leaving Matt to follow the driver down to the street. First the driver pulled some leather things from the back of the truck and tossed them onto the partly frozen lawn. Then he dumped out four bales of hay. "You want these in the barn?" he asked. "There's also a bag with I don't know what in it."

Matt nodded. The driver dragged everything to the concrete entrance to the garage part of the barn. He ripped off a copy of the paper Matt had signed and stuffed it into the bag.

Jerry came tearing back. He was breathless. His parents had gone back to bed, Missy with them, and now all three were asleep. At least his dad said they would be if Jerry would only leave them alone.

The driver went to the rear of the trailer, unlatched and opened a small door at the top, and then lowered the back so that it became a ramp. After that he unclipped a bar and reached inside. The boys heard stamping and shuffling and then saw the horse emerge, head low, ears forward. It stepped with care until all four feet were planted on the street. Then it shook itself.

The driver handed the end of the halter rope to Matt. "I'm out of here," he said as he turned back to raise the ramp. "Oh, and there's this other sack," the driver called over to Matt. "I almost forgot." Reaching into the truck, he hauled out a duffel bag. "Don't know what's in this either," he said, letting it drop to the curb. Then he was inside the truck cab and starting up the engine, pulling away from the curb.

Matt and Jerry stood there with the horse, which didn't seem to care that it was being left behind as the truck backed the trailer into the driveway and then headed out Plympton Street.

12 | MATT WAS TOO stunned to move.

Jerry walked all the way around the horse and then back. He reported his findings: "He's a he. He looks sort of like a pony. His tail is good and long, but his mane's funny; it sticks up. His color changes."

Matt gazed at the horse. It looked right back at him out of dark, wide-set eyes. Matt was afraid to move any closer. He wasn't afraid of the horse. He was afraid that if he touched it, it might vanish like a dream. Not it. He. A boy horse with a coat the color of ashes shading into sooty gray.

"What are you going to do with him?" Jerry asked.

Matt couldn't think. This was different from making a corral out of chairs for Midnight. This was a living, breathing horse that might not want to go into the stall at the back of the barn. Could Matt make him? Should he force him against his will? The horse looked very strong.

Matt tried to recall all the movies he'd ever seen where someone led a horse somewhere. People always seemed to expect the horse to follow willingly. Matt thought he ought to say something to the horse, though, and not just tug him. So he said, "Here, boy, come," the way people speak to dogs. The horse just went on looking at him.

Matt stepped closer to the horse. Now he had to look up to see him. The horse had to look down to see Matt. Then the horse lowered his head and stretched his soot gray muzzle out toward the boy. Without thinking whether he should or shouldn't, Matt freed one hand from the rope and raised it to meet the face that reached toward him. He felt the soft, seeking edge of the horse's nose; warm breath moistened Matt's hand. Now the air he breathed was horse air.

Turning, and without looking back, he started across the lawn to the driveway that led to the barn. He could hear and feel and smell the horse that followed along as though they had always walked together like this, Matt and the horse.

Jerry ran ahead to clear away fresh clutter already building up in the space the boys had cleared. He pulled the stall door wide. Matt led the horse inside. Here, with walls close around them, Matt felt the horse's bulk. That was a little uncomfortable. He wasn't sure about standing right up against the horse to undo the halter rope.

"Come and hold him," Matt said to Jerry.

"No way," Jerry told him. "He's big."

"But he's gentle," Matt said. "Look." And to prove his point, he went right under the horse's chin where he could fumble with the snap hook to get it unlatched.

The horse stood quietly while Matt unhooked the rope. Then, freed, the horse leaned down and rubbed the side of his head against his leg. Matt joined Jerry at the stall door.

"Now what?" asked Jerry.

Matt shook his head. The fact of the horse was so overwhelming that it was hard to think about what he ought to be doing.

"He might be hungry," Jerry said. "He might be thirsty."

Matt nodded. "You stay here. I'll get hay."

"What if he starts to come out?"

"He won't."

"How can you tell?" Jerry asked.

"Well, look at him. Doesn't he look happy?"

The horse shook himself. He stretched out his neck, arched it, and made a face. Then he backed against the wall and rubbed his rump, making a swishing sound as he shifted his weight from one hind leg to the other.

"See?" said Matt. "He feels at home."

Jerry considered this before answering. "You stay. I'll get the hay."

In the end it took both of them to tug the hay string off the bale. Then each of them carried a slab of hay back to the stall. The door was still ajar. The horse had not pushed at it. But as soon as the boys arrived with hay, he stepped forward eagerly.

Jerry dropped his hay and retreated. Matt eyed the hayrack and decided it looked too high to pitch the hay into. So he set his hay down beside Jerry's. The horse didn't seem to mind eating off the floor.

"Now water," Jerry said. But that meant going all the way back to the house for the pail and filling it there. They shut the stall door and slid the bolt to lock it.

They didn't speak as they left the barn. They were too full of amazement, not only because the horse was here but because they were managing things the way people who have horses to care for make sure that whatever needs doing is done.

13 | SERENA WAS IN the kitchen. When the boys brought the pail over to the sink, she said to Jerry, "I should've known you were mixed up in all that racket. What got you up so early? And why didn't you stay home?" She turned to Matt. "What are you doing with that bucket?" she demanded.

"It's for water," he said. "It's for the horse. It came."

"Well, you can just pretend water," she told him. "I don't feel like mopping up after you kids."

"I won't spill any," Matt said as the water splashed too hard and went all over the counter. He turned the faucet down. "It has to be real," he informed her, wondering how much water a horse might drink.

"Where are you going with it?" she snapped as Matt struggled to lift the half-full pail up over the rim of the sink. "Do your parents let you do this sort of thing?"

Grunting, Matt nodded.

"You're not fooling around with water in your room?"

"Of course he's not taking it to his room," Jerry told her. "Gramma, it's for his horse."

"Oh, you two," she complained, but she helped lower the pail to the floor.

Linda came in, yawning. "What's up?" she asked. "What was all that noise about? I was going to sleep late."

"The horse," Matt told her. "How come you didn't get up to see?"

Linda shrugged. "It might've been someone breaking in. I figured Serena should check first since she's here to keep us safe." Turning, still yawning, Linda shuffled back down the hall.

Matt struggled to keep the water from sloshing, but even before he got the pail out of the kitchen, there was a trail of water on the floor.

"Go on," Serena told him. "Just go."

By the time the boys reached the stall, there was only about a quarter of a pail of water left. When they opened the stall door, the horse stepped right over his hay to meet them and thrust his nose down inside the pail. The boys could hear him gulping and slurping. In less than a minute the pail was empty. The horse shoved it so hard that he pushed Matt backward. Then he raised his head and gave Matt a thirsty look.

"Anyway," Jerry said consolingly, "he's still got plenty of hay left."

Yes, thought Matt. But that was the easy part. Now he had to start all over with the water. He imagined trip after trip from the kitchen to the barn, each leaving its spill and making Serena madder. "Maybe you could get your grandmother to go home," he suggested.

Jerry looked doubtful.

"Or keep her busy in the kitchen, and I'll fill the pail in the bathtub."

Back they went, Jerry to tell his gramma how awful Missy had been, Matt to the bathroom. He found out that it was easier to lift the pail out of the tub than out of the kitchen sink. He used both hands, stooping to hold the pail steady as he made his way to the front door.

But Jerry didn't realize that he needed to keep Serena busy for longer than one filling and carrying of the pail. Dashing after Matt, Jerry caught up with him in time to see the horse drink down all the water again.

The two boys regarded the empty pail with dismay. There was only one way out of the problem. This time they went to Jerry's house for water. No one was around to ask questions, so they borrowed the Brewsters' pail, too. Each boy managed to get most of the way to the door before spilling much water. But carrying nearly full pails down the outdoor steps was harder. By the time they made it across the street and up the driveway to the Hoffmans' barn, they were pretty well drenched themselves.

But there was enough water, at least for now. The horse emptied only one of the pails and then sort of played with the water in the second one. Matt left the remaining water just outside the stall so that the horse couldn't knock it over.

The horse rested his chin on the top edge of the door, just where Matt had straddled it when he pounded the horseshoe into the doorpost. Now Matt looked at the horseshoe, the open end up. Maybe he would name the horse Lucky. Only it wasn't just good luck that had brought him here. It was Uncle Oliver, who was far, far away.

Before going to the house for breakfast, which was long overdue, the boys pushed and shoved the bales of hay inside the barn and against the wall so they wouldn't be in the way of the car. Then they gathered up the other stuff the truck driver had left, including Uncle Oliver's duffel bag, and dragged them way back to the corridor between the stalls.

That done, they decided that everything was in order. Matt's shoulder ached from hauling all those pails, but he felt terrific. Here was his horse, looking content now, maybe even glad to be out of the trailer and in a big, peaceful stall with a boy to bring him water.

Where had the horse come from? How long it had taken for him to get here? Did he have a name already? He must have had one where he lived before, a name that he knew. If Matt found it out, maybe the horse would come to him when he called him.

14 | SERENA FUMED. She told the boys to change into dry clothes. Jerry didn't bother to go home. He and Matt were used to wearing each other's things.

Alan talked grown-up to grown-up with Serena. She didn't have to stay and be driven crazy. He could keep an eye on the kids.

It was at this point that Matt and Jerry came back into the kitchen.

Serena went over and sniffed them. "Better," she declared. "Whatever you were into made you smell awful."

Matt said, "Horses smell. You'll get used to it."

Serena wrinkled her nose and shook her head. "How about you get used to being clean? And dry," she added.

Alan said, "Serena, really, don't worry. Dad and Mom will be back in a few hours."

So Serena packed her overnight bag and went home. Matt and Jerry toasted frozen waffles. They asked Alan when he was going to go to the barn to see the horse.

"Not now," he told them. "You two can fool around there if you don't make a mess. I have to write a book report, and I haven't even finished the book."

"It's not fooling around," Matt said.

"I know," Alan responded, sounding just like Mom. Matt tried Linda. "Want to come see my horse?"

"Sure," she said, starting for his room.

"In the barn," Matt said.

Linda was very nice about it. "Maybe later. I have to wash my hair. Your horse will still be there, won't it?"

"Of course," Matt told her. "It's a he."

"Okay, then. He. You two have fun with him." And she closed herself into the bathroom.

Matt and Jerry went back to the barn. The horse seemed glad to see them. Maybe he was bored. Maybe he was thirsty. Matt offered him water, but he didn't drink any. There was a pile of manure over in the corner of his stall. Matt wasn't sure what to do about it.

"The trapdoor," Jerry said.

But if they shoveled the manure down through, it would land on the neatly stacked wood.

They went around to the back of the barn and scrambled up the woodpile, which wasn't nearly so neat or so big as it had been when they'd looked at it in January. They spent the next hour or so moving the wood, heaping it on either side of the space under the trapdoor. Finally they cleared enough of an area so that they could set the two-wheeled garden cart right below the trapdoor.

Back they went to the front of the barn. First they had to raise the trapdoor. Next Matt grabbed a shovel and headed for the stall. But the horse was ready to come out now. They had to shut the door in his face. Then Matt got the rope and slipped inside the stall. He still had a little trouble with the snap hook, but he managed to get the horse on the rope and the rope through the ring in the wall. He tied quite a few knots, which used up most of the rope. The horse rolled his eyes at Matt and looked annoyed.

"It's only for a minute," Matt told him.

It took four shovel trips before the pile in the corner of the stall was gone. By then there was a fresh pile just behind the tied horse. Matt stared at it. At this rate the entire stall floor would be covered with poop by the time he got home from school tomorrow.

As he started shoveling again, it occurred to him that the garden cart might be more useful if he wheeled it right into the stall. Maybe he could find something else to put under the floor for the manure to drop into.

The boys looked everywhere. The barrels were too big and heavy to move. Matt pulled open the drawers in a filing cabinet. But whoever had filled those drawers with manila folders might object to their being emptied out. Plant trays were too shallow and small. The wading pool looked promising, and it weighed practically nothing.

When the boys got back to the underside of the barn, they found that some of the manure had not landed in the garden cart. Jerry was on his way to get the shovel when his father called from the street.

"We're here!" Matt responded. "Come see the horse."

"I need Jerry. We're supposed to be at his aunt's for Sunday dinner."

So Jerry dropped the shovel through the hatch and ran down the driveway to join his father.

Matt cleaned up around the cart and dragged it out of the way. Then he set the wading pool in place. After wheeling the cart to the far end of the garden, he dumped the manure beside last fall's rotting leaves. Then he took the cart and shovel around to the front of the barn and left them by the stall for the next cleanup.

The horse nudged the door. He stamped one foot, sort of kicking against the wall.

Matt longed to take him out to stretch his legs. But what if he pulled free? Matt didn't think the horse would mean to run away. Still, if a car scared him or if a barking dog dashed up to him, anything could happen.

By now Matt was hungry again. That made him think

the horse might want more hay. So he brought him some and offered him a drink. The horse drained the pail.

Matt didn't really mind. He was willing to work all day for the horse if he had to. It was just hard to picture tomorrow and the day after that.

When he carried the two pails into the house, Linda called to him from the kitchen to ask if he wanted any soup.

"In a minute," he told her as he headed for the bathroom. He figured that if he filled each pail only partway, maybe he could carry both at once, and without spilling. This system worked. The only problem was that he didn't end up with enough water. After letting the horse drink his fill, Matt had to make another trip to the house. By the time he was finished, Linda was gone from the kitchen.

Matt found the soup cooling on the stove. He ladled some into a bowl, and then, without even bothering with a spoon, he drank it all down. Like the horse, Matt thought, feeling as if they shared a common thirst.

Too tired to think of eating, he staggered off to his room, where he stood for a long moment gazing at Midnight and the other horses on his shelf. They were different now. They were made of wood and plastic.

They had no smell, no warmth, no energy.

But he felt funny turning away from them. So he picked up Midnight and took him over to the bed. There was the book Matt had been reading last night. Not a very good story, but with wonderful pictures of a horse named Blaze. Matt's head dropped down onto the open book. Reaching out for Midnight, Matt sank into a deep, dreamless sleep.

15 | MATT AWOKE WITH a start. There was a stir out in the hall, voices raised just beyond his door. Something must have happened. Still in the grip of sleep, he couldn't think what time it was, let alone what day.

Then, very clearly, he heard his mother's voice. All in a rush it came to him: This was Saturday; Mom and Dad were home. There was something more. Raising himself, he looked down on the open book and saw the picture. In a single instant his heart leaped and then tumbled. He had fallen asleep over the picture of Blaze and had dreamed that a real horse had come. A horse the color of ashes and soot with a thick black-and-white tail and a stand-up mane. What a dream!

It wasn't until he swung his legs over the side of the bed and saw that he was fully dressed that the dream horse rearranged itself in his mind. Slowly. He stared at flecks of hayseed on his pants. He examined his sneakers, a few telltale smudges just above the soles. He didn't have to smell them to know what they had been into. Anyway, horse scent was on his hands, too. Bringing them to his face, he inhaled deeply.

Now he looked at his clock. It was just past four, which meant that he had hardly slept at all. How weird to have so much trouble waking up. Maybe because he wasn't used to sleeping in the middle of the day like a baby, like Missy.

He walked to his door. When he opened it, Mom looked up from something she was showing Linda and gave him a big smile.

"It's so good to be home," she declared. "I missed you."

"Maybe Matt can clear up the mystery," Dad said.

Mystery? Matt didn't know about any mystery.

"The holes," Dad said, opening the front door and pointing past the driveway.

Then Matt noticed the holes in the partly frozen ground. They made a pattern on the lawn all the way down to the street. He couldn't see beyond the car, but he guessed the holes continued on to the barn.

"It must be the horse," he said. "I didn't notice it happening."

"Horse!" said his father. "Those holes look more like the work of a hippopotamus."

Matt was relieved that his father had made a joke. That meant the holes could be fixed and the horse wouldn't be blamed. Matt was also relieved that Dad took the arrival of the horse in stride. Linda and Alan must have broken the news already.

Matt's mother said, "Whatever it was, Matt, it's made a mess of the lawn. You have to be extra-careful this time of year when the frost is coming out of the ground. It's very soft and it's easily damaged. Remember, you're not supposed to ride your bike on it either."

Matt nodded. "I'll keep the horse off it from now on," he answered.

Alan said, "Matt and Jerry have been doing their horse thing all day. I thought they were in the barn."

"We were," Matt said. "Nobody would come to see him."

"See who?" asked Mom.

"The horse."

"Well," said Dad, "you can't expect your brother and sister to be as interested in your projects as your doting parents. Let me put away some of my things, and I'll come out with you." He turned to Alan and Linda. "It wouldn't've hurt you two to show a little more support for your kid brother the first time we were both away."

"Serena was here," Alan reminded him.

"Serena was very kind to help us out," Mom replied. "She has her own family to think about."

Linda didn't try to defend herself. She just pulled on her jacket and asked Matt to show her what he and Jerry had been up to all day with their horse. Just the way she said it showed Matt that she still thought it was a game. So he told her the horse was in his stall and left it at that. With her kind of attitude he didn't care whether she went out to see the horse or not.

He followed his parents upstairs and down the hall to their room. They had brought Matt a present, a model saddle from the display of a dude ranch out West. It was perfect in every detail, even down to the tiny wooden stirrups.

Matt was turning it over and over in his hands when Linda burst into the room.

"Mom!" she shrieked. "Dad! There's a horse in the barn!"

That brought Alan to the door. "Ha, ha!" he said.

"There is!" Linda insisted.

Dad smiled at his children. "All right," he told Linda. "I'll bite. Just let me get changed." He went into the bathroom, leaving Mom to deal with Linda.

"You're good at this," Mom said to her. "You could've convinced me."

"There's a horse," Linda repeated. "Honestly."

Matt said nothing. But he noticed that Alan slipped away without a word.

While Mom changed into jeans and a turtleneck, Linda sidled over to Matt. He dropped his eyes to the saddle.

"Hey, Matt," she said, "I thought it was just your usual stuff, you know. That's what it sounded like."

Matt raised his eyes and met hers. "Isn't he beautiful?" he asked.

"I guess. I was so surprised I didn't really—"

"Mom!" Alan was back. "Man!" he said.

Mom, leaning over to tie her sneaker laces, said, "What?" Then she straightened. "Oh. You're in on this, too?"

"No. Yes. It's true."

Dad appeared, ready to go out with Matt, and stopped short. "Isn't this joke wearing a little thin?" he said. "I'm not sure it's funny anymore."

"It never was," said Matt.

Suddenly he was the center of attention. No one spoke. They just fixed him with intense looks.

Matt drew a breath, but he had nothing more to say. The time had come for his whole family to meet his horse.

16

"WHY IS EVERYONE so surprised?" Matt asked.

His family stood gaping at the horse. No one answered him.

Finally Matt's father spoke. "Who put it here?" There was hardly any voice behind his words.

"I did," Matt said. "He's a he," he added. "He needed to go somewhere. And the stall was ready for him."

"He's pretty big," said Linda. "Did you have any trouble?"

Matt shook his head. "He let me tie him up, too. He didn't like it, but he let me."

"Great heavens!" Mom gasped. "You don't know anything about him. He could've stepped on you."

Matt shook his head. "He's not like that. You'll see." He picked up the halter rope and opened the stall door just wide enough to slip inside.

"Matt, no!" cried his father.

"It's all right." Matt attached the rope to the halter and shoved the door wide. "Now you can get a good look at him."

But instead of coming closer, the family stepped back a little.

Matt's father shook his head. "How could he?" he whispered. "How could Oliver do this to us?"

"It's not *to you*, Dad," Matt explained. "It's *for me*. Uncle Oliver promised."

Silence greeted this statement.

Matt said. "I always knew he would send my horse."

But Dad was looking at Mom, whose glance slid back and forth between him and the horse. "Was there a phone call or anything?" she finally asked.

"He just came," Matt said. He added that he thought the driver of the truck that pulled the trailer was just delivering the horse. "He left some other stuff, too," Matt added.

The horse pricked his ears forward. Standing beside him, Matt saw that he was looking expectantly at the entire Brewster family coming into the barn. Jerry led them proudly to the stall. Jerry's mother carried Missy, who was asleep on her shoulder.

"We couldn't wait to get home," she said. "We were

visiting family. Jerry broke the news at dinner."

Leroy walked right past everyone and into the stall. He touched the horse, then ran his hand down the side of the animal's neck. "Unusual," Leroy murmured. "He's so sturdy, like a pony. Built for work."

"Fine," Matt's father declared. "Have you any suggestions for finding him a job?"

"What kind of job?" Matt asked.

"Honestly, Ellie," Serena was saying, "I never dreamed the boys were talking about a real horse."

"Well," Matt's mother answered, "if you didn't see it arrive, how could you have guessed? We didn't catch on either. And, Serena, we can't thank you enough for staying here."

Now the two fathers were conferring. "There ought to be an envelope or something," Matt's father said. "Who signed for the beast?"

"He's not a beast," Matt said. "I signed. Can we take him outdoors? Can we take him for a walk?"

"Good heavens, no!" Dad exclaimed. "What if he messes in front of someone's house?"

Alan laughed. "We'll need a pretty big pooper-scooper."

"But Matt's right," Linda said. "You can see he wants to get out. Is there a law against horses? Didn't people used to have them right in this barn?"

"And in our house, too," Jerry told her. "My room upstairs was a hayloft. Right, Dad?"

Leroy nodded. "But times have changed. So have zoning laws."

"Well," Mom pointed out, "the horse won't be here long enough to get people stirred up. Maybe we should give him a chance to stretch his legs."

"What do you mean?" Matt demanded. "Why won't he be?"

"Oh, Matt." Mom shook her head. "We can't keep a horse."

That statement brought an outcry from all the kids, including Alan. How could the grown-ups say that when the horse had just come? It might work out. Anyway, it was Matt's horse. Or Uncle Oliver's. They couldn't just get rid of it.

To Matt's astonishment the grown-ups backed down. For now. They said the usual grown-up things about looking into the situation, making informed decisions, and facing reality.

Then everyone stepped aside as Matt led the horse out of the stall. Jerry walked on one side, his hand on the horse's shoulder, while Matt, rope in hand, walked on the other.

Outside, the horse moved with more vigor. He took Matt by surprise. First the horse went after the dead grass at the edge of the driveway. When Matt hauled him back, the horse veered. Dragging Matt along, the horse lurched toward a barberry bush. He began to nibble its leafless, prickly branches.

Alan and Linda ran to help. Together they tugged the horse away from the shrub. It was clear that Matt wasn't able to take the horse for a walk by himself.

As they headed down to the street, Mom shouted after them to remember to keep the horse off all lawns. They were too busy working out the rules for the walk to call back to her, but they heard. Matt promised himself that he would fix the holes in his lawn as soon as he got back from the horse's outing.

Meanwhile they had the horse to attend to, each one taking a turn with the rope, but with Alan at its bitter end in case the horse broke away. To Matt, it felt like being at the head of a parade. People came out of their houses to stare at the small procession. Pretty soon kids on bikes and skateboards and Rollerblades were tagging along or wheeling ahead to announce the coming of the horse.

And what a sight he made, thought Matt, who ran all around to get a good look at him. From uphill Matt

was able to see the dark stripe that ran from the horse's two-tone mane all the way down his back to his tail. Matt also noticed thinner stripes across the legs. These stripes blurred as the gray coloring deepened down the legs. The horse was one shade on top, another on the bottom. Yet it all matched; even the shading on his face darkened to the muzzle.

The horse seemed to enjoy the attention as well as the exercise. He swished his tail and held his broad head high. The thick forelock parted as he thrust forward, the black and white strands mingling. He snorted and seemed almost to dance.

When Matt took another turn with the lead rope and speeded up, the horse broke into a trot and pulled ahead. This time, even though Alan was ready to help, Matt only had to speak to the horse to slow him down.

17

ALAN SAID, "This is bad. We left all the parents together by themselves."

"Why is that bad?" asked Matt as he held the water bucket steady for the horse.

"They wanted us out of the way while they figured out how to get rid of him."

"Mom and Dad wouldn't do anything that sneaky," Linda retorted.

"Right," Alan said in a tone that meant "wrong." "How much do you want to bet they're sitting around plotting right now?"

"Let's go see," said Jerry.

"First, I need to bring more water." Matt told them. "It takes lots of trips."

Alan grabbed the other bucket. Then halfway to the house he stopped and asked Matt where he was getting the water from. When Matt told him, Alan groaned. "Doofus," he said, "didn't you ever think of the hose? I guess I'm going to have to be the brains of this project." He turned back to the barn.

"I can be the brains," Linda told him. "You're never around."

"You're second-in-command," Alan said.

They both glanced at Matt, but he had nothing to say. They could fight over being the brains for all he cared. He knew he was the heart of it all.

They had to hunt awhile before they could find the hose coiled neatly among cold frames and pots. Alan explained to everyone that for the next few weeks the hose would have to be drained in case it froze at night.

After the water pails were filled, one left in the stall and one outside it, the kids joined the parents in the

Hoffmans' living room. Serena had taken Missy home. That left four grown-ups, who had had a head start, and four kids, more united than usual.

"How did the walk go?" Dad asked.

"Fine," Matt promptly answered, eager to show how easy it was to take care of his horse.

"The horse went to the bathroom in front of Mrs. Dworkin's house," Jerry said. "And guess what?"

Matt's father groaned. "She's suing us?"

"No," Linda told him. "She asked us to shovel it onto her flower bed. She's not ready to dig it in yet. She said she'll pay us a dollar for every bushel of manure we deliver to her. What's a bushel?"

"We said we would," Alan added, "but we told her she might have to share with some of the other neighbors later on."

The parents exchanged glances.

Still anxious to reassure them, Matt said, "We already decided that anything we make goes to the horse. For food and stuff."

A long silence followed this news. Matt had a good feeling about the situation. They had already started to look into it. They had already made an informed decision. And surely they had shown that they were facing reality.

Jerry's father said, "Why don't we tell you some of what we found out about this animal?" He nodded at

Matt's mother and father, urging them with a look to sort of change the subject.

Mom started to explain that they had discovered papers in the bag with the name and address of the distant farm where the horse had come from. "There's a vet's health certificate, a brochure, a registration, and other information. This is a very special kind of horse. I mean, Uncle Oliver clearly meant well."

Matt's father made a rude noise. "If buying a valuable animal for a child who couldn't possibly keep him is meaning well."

Everyone burst out at once. But it was Leroy, used to making himself heard over a school clamor, who managed to take the lead. "Look, this will all get sorted out," he declared. "No doubt that farm will take him back."

"Even if they will," Jerry's mother argued, "someone's going to have to fork out a heap of money to get the horse trucked all the way back there. It's out of state."

"Right, Trish," Matt's mother said. "My point exactly."

"Where?" asked Matt, eager to learn more about his horse. "What state?"

But the answer that came from Matt's father was buried by Leroy's astonishing statement that the horse came from Norway.

"Norway, the country?" Linda exclaimed.

"From Europe?" Alan demanded.

"Cool!" said Jerry. "Where's Norway?"

"Sorry," Leroy told them. "I mean the breed is from Norway. It's called a Norwegian Fjord horse. I've only just glanced at the material, but it's kind of interesting. The Fjord horse is a dual-purpose animal that—"

"What does that mean, 'dual purpose'?" Matt interrupted.

"It's for both riding and pulling. That's why it looks like a small draft horse. They're supposed to be easy to train and inexpensive to keep if—"

"Easy, Leroy," Matt's father said. "You're beginning to sound like a promoter."

"But look"—Jerry's father went on—"the kids might as well know all this. Ellie's uncle must have gone to some trouble to locate this horse. Maybe we can find out why he chose such an uncommon breed."

"Knowing Oliver," muttered Matt's father, "I'd guess it could have been a passing impulse."

"That's not fair," Mom declared. "You've no idea what he had in mind."

"Why not ask him?" Trish suggested.

"Wouldn't I like to," Matt's father replied. "But our uncle Oliver has got himself even farther away than Norway. He's unreachable."

"In Tasmania," Alan added.

Matt leaned back against the window and listened to the conversation veer away from the question of what was to become of his horse. Leroy got so excited talking about the possibility of discovering a living Tasmanian tiger that the horse seemed forgotten. Pretty soon Trish stood up and said they should be getting home.

After the Brewsters left, Matt's mother remarked to Matt's father that maybe he should think again about a wildlife tour in some remote region. People like Leroy might be willing to spring for the vacation of a lifetime.

"There aren't many people like Leroy, not here in Marbury," he replied. "Anyway, we still have to deal with the problem your uncle dumped on us."

"I know," she said. "But we can't solve it today."

The three children drifted upstairs to Alan's room. Matt started out being careful about the imaginary line from last fall, but soon he forgot about it because Alan didn't seem to care anymore.

"Maybe we should get in touch with Uncle Oliver," Linda said.

Alan shook his head. "We can't wait for him to help us. The problem is the cost of keeping the horse. We have to raise some money."

"We'll have the manure to sell," Matt reminded him.

"That's probably not enough. We have to think big."

Matt nodded. But right now he could barely think beyond the next pail of water. Then he remembered that the hose was hooked up. Maybe, thought Matt, he should stick to small matters for now and count on Alan and Linda for the brainy stuff. And Leroy. For it was just beginning to dawn on Matt that Jerry's father didn't seem so firmly lined up with the other grown-ups against the horse. If the kids had Leroy on their side, they might even have a chance.

18 | MATT WAS ON to something, but Alan warned him to cool it. The only way to get Leroy Brewster to stick up for the horse was to let him reach his own conclusions.

"Yes," Linda said, "but the horse is where he wants to keep an emu."

They pondered this conflict. Then Alan came up with a plan. If they all got interested in emus, maybe Leroy would get involved with the horse.

But Jerry's father was way ahead of them. He showed up after supper with Marianne from Wilmot Place. According to Leroy, she was an expert. Not an expert exactly, she said, but she had worked with horses. So the Hoffmans trooped out to the barn with her.

She took her time looking over the horse and the things that had been delivered with him. "He's in excellent shape," she declared. Matt's heart soared. "Nice size, too. The build of a pony with the temperament of a horse."

"He is a horse!" Matt blurted.

Marianne nodded. "Yes and no. Strictly speaking, he measures pony height. But you're right. He's a horse as far as the breed goes." She turned to Matt's parents. "You'll need bedding. You can't keep a horse in a stall without bedding."

"We're not keeping a horse," Matt's father told her. "It's just until—"

"This is important," said Marianne. "Straw or wood shavings," she told him firmly. "There's a riding stable outside town that'll sell you a few bales."

"Who's paying?" asked Matt's father.

The children glanced at one another. "We will," Linda said.

"For now," Alan added. "When we start selling the manure, the horse will pay."

"He'll need a place to get out. It's not fair to confine him," Marianne went on. "Some place fenced and safe."

No one answered her. The children were trying to

think of such a place. The parents were thinking their own private thoughts.

"Like the old graveyard off Lookout Drive," Marianne suggested. "It has a gate that shuts and the high wall."

"And gravestones," Dad remarked. "Can you imagine what people would say?"

"They wouldn't have to mow the grass," Alan pointed out. "That would save the town of Marbury a lot of money. They ought to be glad to have a horse there."

"Don't even mention the possibility," said Mom. "Not to anyone."

"Well, there's always the riding stable. I don't suppose you'd want to board the horse. They might give you a good deal if you made him available for renting out."

"No way." Matt objected. "We're not renting my horse. Or sending him away. He has a perfectly good stall here."

"Cool it," Alan muttered.

"We can't get into this now," Dad said grimly. "We've been away. We just got home."

Marianne gave Leroy directions to the riding stable. She wished everyone luck. Then, just as she turned to leave, she said, "I'd love to have him at Wilmot Place. But we're on a tight budget, and even with our special permit we have to keep our numbers low. The trustees rarely approve a new animal, even an endangered one."

Matt glanced at his parents, who didn't look defeated exactly, just worn out. He knew that wouldn't last. He knew they intended to get rid of the horse as soon as they could figure out how to. He felt like telling Marianne that this horse was endangered.

As soon as she took off, Matt's parents headed back to the house. Jerry's father seemed a little surprised to find himself the only one left to drive to the stable for bedding. The kids, who had no idea what the straw would cost, went to get money. Then they all piled into the Brewsters' van.

Alan asked Leroy about emus. Pretty soon they were talking about Uncle Oliver's current adventure on the island of Tasmania, which happened to be the original home not only of emus but of all kinds of other unusual species. Leroy was so caught up in explaining the difference between rare and endangered animals that he would have driven right past the riding stable if Jerry and Matt hadn't yelled at him to stop.

Matt's heart sank at the sight of all the fences, all the safe places for horses that didn't have to be tied up. In one of the outlying paddocks foals galloped around in circles and kicked up their heels. The mother horses stood placidly watching, like slightly bored parents at a playground keeping an eye on unruly children. "Let's ask what it costs to keep a horse here," he whispered to Jerry.

They spoke with a man inside the stable. "If we kept our horse here," Jerry said, "would it be very expensive?"

"Are you serious?" asked the man, directing his question at Jerry's father.

"We might as well know," Leroy said, "because sooner or later someone will object to a horse in a residential area and he'll have to be moved."

Everyone gasped when the man told them the monthly rate for boarding a horse. They managed to get two bales of straw into the back of the van and two more bales of hay on the roof rack. They even paid without bothering to count how much each kid put in. But on the trip home no one had much to say.

Matt wondered how something so wonderful as this real horse could become his and become threatened all at the same time. He let out a sigh. What a day it had been, a long day.

Hearing him, Jerry's father said, "We'll figure out something."

We. Leroy really was on the horse's side. A glimmer of hope.

By the time they got home, it was dark. Everyone

helped unload the bales. Matt shoveled manure from the stall into the garden cart, and then they all stood awhile longer, admiring the horse as he snatched hay from the freshly filled rack.

"Loki," murmured Jerry's father.

"What?"

"Loki. That's his name. Didn't anyone tell you?" "Anyone" meant one of Matt's parents.

"You found out his name?" Matt exclaimed in a final burst of excitement.

"It's on all those papers that came with him," Leroy told him.

"Lucky," Matt said, shifting his gaze to the horseshoe nailed to the doorpost. This was more than a gift. The horse he had dreamed of had come with the very name he had chosen. It was almost as if he had known right along who the horse would be.

19 BUT THE HORSE'S name was Loki, not Lucky. Matt found out in time for school. So he was able to get everything right when he told the other kids. He didn't mind about the name since it sounded

almost the same. It might even be Norwegian for Lucky.

After school kids who could walk or bike to Plympton Street came to see the horse. They streamed into the barn and had to wait in line for a viewing.

"Charge admission," Jerry whispered to Matt, who returned with the emptied garden cart to find the way to the stall blocked.

But it was too late. Some had already seen Loki for free. It wouldn't be fair to the ones still waiting. Besides, they wouldn't have come with money.

"And you don't want to turn kids against Loki," Linda pointed out. "We need them on our side." She thought a moment. "But it's not a bad idea. Maybe we can give them something to do, something fun that they have to pay for."

All afternoon the stall door had to remain open. Patiently Loki stood tied to the ring while Matt and Jerry and Linda took turns brushing him and various friends begged for a chance to help.

Afterward Linda made a sign-up schedule on posterboard. It took a couple of days to complete, because no one could agree on what to charge a kid for grooming Loki or holding his halter rope for part of his afternoon walk.

By the end of the week most of the kids had stopped

coming. That left a hard-core group of loyal fans, not all girls, who still showed up to work or just hang out around Loki. Their parents began to call Matt's parents. Music lessons had been cut, karate classes bypassed, softball practice missed, baby-sitting forgotten, dentist appointments ignored. The dentist charged for the appointment, anyway. It was hinted that since this was the Hoffmans' fault, they should pay the bill.

Alan demanded to know how Loki could be a self-supporting horse if they weren't allowed to collect money from people who were willing to pay for the fun of grooming and walking him. Mom and Dad talked about the high cost of insurance they would need in case a child was injured.

"Loki wouldn't hurt anyone," Matt told them. "He likes the kids."

"Even so," Dad said, "if someone's hurt in our barn or with your horse, we can be sued for more than a dentist visit."

Linda, who had brought a riding schedule on paper to show Mom and Dad, backed off. Slowly she folded the paper into a small enough square to shove into her pocket.

Mom repeated what she had been saying all along about Uncle Oliver. He didn't understand the limits of a town like Marbury. He didn't know a thing about residential zoning. Probably it had never occurred to him that Matt couldn't keep a horse here.

"Probably it never occurred to him to include a bundle of money in his marvelous gift," Dad added.

"But we shouldn't forget that he meant well," Mom said. "And, Matt, you ought to write and thank him."

"I thought he couldn't be reached," Alan declared.

Mom nodded. "Still, Matt should thank him. Sooner or later Uncle Oliver will get the letter. He'll see that Matt wrote promptly."

A long silence followed. Then Mom went on to say that she and Dad had already been in touch with the farm Loki had come from. It would cost a great deal to ship him back. The ideal solution would be to find someone around here who wanted a Fjord horse. The farm was looking into that possibility.

Matt scowled. "I can't thank Uncle Oliver if I don't have Loki."

"You thank him for the gift," Mom said. "For the thought."

"Forget the thought," Dad muttered. "I'm with Matt on that."

For one glorious moment Matt believed that Dad meant he wanted Loki to stay. Then Mom reminded

Dad that no one should look a gift horse in the mouth. They burst out laughing as if she had made a joke, and it was clear they were on the same side again. Or still.

Matt and Linda and Alan, who were not laughing, went out and gathered in front of Loki's stall to wait for Marianne. She was coming to try out some things with the horse, mostly to do with riding.

Of course Matt had been sitting astride him in the stall. Loki hadn't seemed to mind at all. Matt could even stretch out flat or else swivel around and sit back to front while he brushed Loki's rump. Still, he couldn't wait for a real ride.

20

GETTING ONTO LOKI outside wasn't anything like being in the stall. Without an overturned bucket for Matt to step on, Jerry's father had to lift him onto the horse's back. At first it was jarring, unsettling. Matt leaned forward to grab the stiff, upright mane, but there wasn't enough of it to hold. Marianne set a hard hat on his head. Then, when she began to lead Loki down Plympton Street, Matt responded to the rhythm of the horse's stride and was able to straighten and clutch the warm, rounded body with his legs.

Marianne, who had scouted out the neighorhood with Jerry's father, chose the empty lot next to the ball field. The ground was sort of gravelly with dead weeds and a few skeletal bushes. Matt slid off Loki's back. Everyone except Alan, who said he had something else to do, had to look around for broken glass and drink cans.

After an area was cleared, Marianne clipped a long canvas line to the halter, removed the lead rope, stepped away from everyone, and let the horse start to walk around her. Almost at once the horse broke into a trot. She made clucking sounds, let out more line, and then let him take off in circles. Arching his thick neck, he dipped his muzzle to his knees and then thrust it high, high up. Suddenly he was twisting and bucking and kicking up his heels. She let him go around and around like this until he slowed of his own accord. Then she walked to him and stroked and patted him.

"He needed that," she told the watchers, who still gaped with surprise at Loki's wildness. "Now the opposite direction," she declared, starting him around her the other way. She made him trot and then canter. He performed a few halfhearted kicks, then moved from a canter to trot and back to a canter. Finally she slowed him and made him walk quietly.

Matt could still feel the energy and joy that had come

into Loki when he let loose. He might be small like a pony, but his spirit was huge. For the first time Matt felt doubt creep through him. He had been thinking so hard about winning over Mom and Dad that he hadn't really come to grips with what life in Marbury would be like for Loki. All at once the prospect of keeping the horse seemed overwhelming.

Then Marianne put a bridle on Loki. She spent a long time adjusting straps to make it fit. After donning the hard hat, she sprang up and swung her leg over Loki's back. There she sat, feeling him the way Matt had in the stall. "I'm not used to this," she said, laughing a little. Then she urged Loki forward.

"He seems well mannered," Jerry's father remarked.

"What about all that bucking?" Linda asked.

Leroy shrugged. "I suppose that's what he'd do if he went free. But look how nice he's being with Marianne."

The horse turned, trotted slowly, walked again, turned once more. After a while Marianne brought him back to the watchers. Sliding off his back, she removed her hard hat and held it out to Matt. "Your turn?" she asked.

"Do I have to wear this here?" he asked, glancing over at the ball field to see if any of the older boys were watching. He wished he had brought his cowboy hat.

"Yes. Or a bike helmet. Anytime you ride. All of you

do," she said, turning to the others as she put the halter on over the bridle with the long canvas line attached. As soon as Leroy boosted Matt onto Loki's back, she started the horse walking around at the end of the line.

Half expecting him to start bucking again, Matt grabbed the reins.

"Those are for later," she told him. "Keep them loose now."

Nodding, too excited to speak, he loosened the reins and concentrated on what was happening with Loki.

As it turned out, not much was happening. Marianne wanted to take things easy this first time. Besides, everyone else was waiting for a turn. So Matt had to pretend that Loki was galloping. He leaned as he imagined what a gallop felt like, lost his balance, and fell to the ground.

He didn't have far to go. He could see the clear advantage of a small horse. But he did land on his rear end, which made him feel like some dumb kid in a cartoon. At least no one made fun of him. Marianne made sure he was okay and then paid no more attention to the fall. Matt didn't exactly claim that he had fallen on purpose, but he did say that it was important to learn how to fall from a horse to do rodeo tricks.

After each of the remaining kids had a brief ride, Marianne showed them how to use the long line to exercise Loki. Right from the start Linda managed to hold the coiled line in one hand while handling the horse with the other. Marianne said she was a natural.

Matt tried so hard to copy her that he wrapped the line around himself until he looked like a cocoon. Loki just stopped, looking puzzled when he ran out of line. Marianne told Matt to remember to turn with the horse. She said he could borrow the line, and if he practiced, he'd soon catch on.

Jerry, who had decided not to try the line today, got to sit on Loki's back for the walk home. Matt kept running ahead and around just to see Loki from every angle. He loved the way the horse walked with his whole body, from nodding head to swishing tail. He loved the way Loki's ears pricked at things that caught his attention. Most of all he loved the way Loki cast his eyes on Matt as if he already knew him.

Marianne promised to come again when she had some spare time. She told the kids that in the meantime they should read about horses and riding. They needed to learn how to cool him down and clean his hooves. The closer they got to home, the more she sounded like a teacher. She got Jerry's father going again about Norwegian Fjord horses. He invited the kids over to look at a book with pictures of rare and extinct horses.

So after they had put Loki away in his big, clean stall, Matt and Linda and Jerry went for a sort of science lesson, each of them mindful of how much Jerry's father had already done for the horse and might yet do to help them keep him.

21]

Dear Uncle Oliver,

Thank you for Loki. I am lucky to have him. Even though some people think he is a pony, I know he is a real horse. I had my first ride. He is smart and he likes me. I like him a lot. I might teach him tricks. I never saw a horse with stripes before. Leroy says Loki is rare but not endangered. He doesn't mind that Loki is in the stall he wants to use for his emu. Did you see an emu yet? Did you find a Tasmanian tiger? We all hope you do so that it isn't extinct.

Love,
Matthew Hoffman

It took Matt days to get the letter written. On Saturday afternoon, when Matt showed it to his mother, she tried to talk to him about finding a new home for Loki.

"But why?" he cried. "It's working out."

"It can't," she told him. "Anyway, not for long. Even if we could afford to keep him, we're not allowed to."

"But no one's complained." He had just had another session with Marianne, who was teaching him how to get Loki trotting and cantering around him in circles. Matt had felt like a circus ringmaster as the horse responded. People in the ball field had wandered over to the fence to watch. Afterward Matt had led Loki right up to them so that they could touch him through the chain links. "Everyone likes him," Matt insisted. "Can't you just leave us alone?"

Mom sighed. "I'm sorry," she told him. "Really, Matt."

"You're not!" he blurted. "You just say you're sorry. You don't want him. You don't want me to have him. You never did." He broke off, breathless and astonished. His outburst brought Alan to the kitchen.

It took Mom a moment to find an answer. She had to set a new tone. "I don't blame you for being angry," she told Matt. "But remember it's not my fault, this horse."

"What's fault got to do with it?" he shouted.

"Hey, Matt!" Alan spoke from the doorway.

Matt still faced his mother. He barely heard Alan's warning. "Try to look beyond the horse problem," Mom was saying.

What problem? he felt like yelling. But the rage had gone out of him now. He was left with a kind of dull ache.

"You've always wanted a dog, right?" Mom continued.

Matt nodded. What did Loki have to do with a dog? Besides, he had never longed for a dog the way he had for a horse.

"Well," Mom said, "your dad and I think you're probably ready to take care of one. And when Loki goes, we can start looking for a dog. How would you like that?"

Matt said, "I don't want Loki to go." Yet he knew that if he could send Loki somewhere that had a fenced field to run in or a big paddock like the one at the stable outside town, he would jump at the chance. It was just that here in the kitchen, with the letter to Uncle Oliver lying beside carrot scrapings and potato peels, he felt cornered. It was almost as though his mother were trying to bribe him with a dog.

Matt picked up the letter. Maybe it was useless to argue. Maybe he should act the way he had when he was waiting for his horse to come. If he just went ahead with Loki from day to day without making waves, maybe the grown-ups would back off.

Matt copied Uncle Oliver's address onto an envelope, put lots of stamps on it because it had so far to go, and then decided to show the letter to Jerry's father.

Alan stopped him in the hall. "You shouldn't lose it like that," he said.

"What difference does it make?" Matt retorted.

"You're always good. It's what they expect. If you start blowing off at them, it'll just convince them the horse is bad for you."

Matt drew a deep breath. "So what can I do?" he asked.

Alan frowned. "I don't know yet. We have to think of something. You can't think unless you keep your cool. So don't get mad. Get even."

But how? wondered Matt. What could a kid like him do to get even? And if he found a way, how would that help him keep Loki?

He walked across the street. Trish and Serena were out shopping. Leroy was home with Jerry and Missy.

"Come on upstairs," Jerry said. "Dad's going to feed Missy. It'll be slime city around here."

Leroy spoke with his head inside the refrigerator. "Look who's talking. What did you do, lie down in Loki's bedding? Go change before your mother and grandmother get back."

As Jerry stumped up the stairs, Matt couldn't help comparing how carefully he always cleaned away all signs and smells of Loki so that Mom and Dad wouldn't notice there was a horse in the barn. Not that it worked.

Leroy mixed some glop and spooned a bit into Missy. She blew it back at him.

"Serena doesn't let her do that," Matt commented.

"My mother's a pro," Leroy responded "She had six kids to practice on before she even started on grandchildren. Now," he added, "if I were an emu, I'd be the natural caregiver for my chick." He let the glop dribble down Missy's front. Then he raised another spoonful to her mouth, which she clamped firmly shut. "In its natural habitat," he told Matt, "the male emu incubates the eggs."

"Is that why you want to hatch one?" Matt asked, backing out of Missy's range when she opened her mouth.

Leroy aimed the spoon at the opening and slid it in, all the while explaining that an emu, the second-largest of all living birds, was friendlier than ostriches. Anyway, emu eggs would be available at Wilmot Place. And if they didn't hatch, he might get another from an emu farm up-country. "The common emu isn't rare. It's all the other emu species that have died out." Thoughtfully Leroy stirred the glop. "Though you never know. Maybe that Tasmanian tiger expedition will come across the extinct Tasmanian emu. That would be exciting, though nothing like discovering the tiger."

Matt remembered that he had come to show Leroy the letter to Uncle Oliver. But he didn't want to get it spattered with glop. "I know they're not really tigers," he said. "I know they're sort of striped wolves. Still, if Uncle Oliver finds one, couldn't it hurt him?"

"The Tasmanian tiger wasn't known for attacking humans," Leroy told him, "even though it was a fierce hunter. It would probably run and hide from people."

Tiger stripes on wolves and zebra stripes on horses. Matt supposed that Uncle Oliver must have had stripes on his mind when he ordered Loki.

Leroy, who was mopping up the high chair tray, talked to Missy as if she could understand every word he said. He tossed the gloppy sponge into the sink and then wiped her face and hands with a dish towel.

"Mom just told me we can't keep Loki," Matt said.

Leroy paused with Missy half lifted from her chair. "Not exactly news," he remarked. "Still, I'm sorry." He hoisted Missy high.

Matt could tell that Leroy really was sorry. It hurt and felt good at the same time.

"I know your folks are sorry, too," Leroy added after a moment. But that was the grown-up in him speaking. It sent a weak shaft of anger through Matt, a shadow of his face-off with Mom. But anger, weak or strong, was useless against the absolute power of grown-ups sticking together.

Seeing that Leroy was no father emu and that Missy was about to be set loose, Matt decided to keep the letter to himself. After all, it was really between Uncle Oliver and him, just as Loki had been from the start.

22 MATT SOON FOUND that Loki invented tricks on his own. When he got bored, he knocked over his plastic pail and kicked it around his stall. Pretty soon the pail got crumpled. Then it was squashed flat. Jerry donated his soccer ball to give Loki something else to kick, but Loki flattened that, too.

Sometimes in the vacant lot he pretended to be startled by a candy wrapper snagged on a bush. Then he would stop short or swerve aside, almost always dumping his rider. He never ran away, though. He would just drop his head to crop the dusty grass that struggled up through the gravel.

But his best—or worst—trick was stealing. While Matt leaned over to pick up manure or to clean Loki's foot, the horse gently nuzzled around the pocket of Matt's jeans until he found something he could tug out. If it was a hoof pick or a comb, something that didn't really interest Loki, he tossed it up in the air and watched Matt scramble to get it back. But if it was a carrot or a marshmallow, Loki always gobbled it right up.

"I would've given it to you, anyway," Matt would scold.

Loki, bobbing his head up and down to place the treat just where he wanted it in his mouth, seemed unaffected by a scolding. He would prick his ears forward, munch contentedly, and show with a certain look that even though he preferred stolen treats, he was now ready to accept some from Matt's hands just to please him.

If only he could get someone like Marianne to help him figure out what to do for Loki.

When Jerry's father went over to Wilmot Place, where he and Marianne were planning a summer nature program, Matt and Jerry went along with him. Matt tried to show an interest in the emus, but he kept glancing away at the fenced field behind the big mansion. Sheep or goats stood at the gate as if they were waiting to come out. Maybe all animals craved to be somewhere else. But Matt had a feeling that if Loki were let go in all that space, he might not have to play so many tricks anymore. Instead he would be happy to run and run until he got himself all tired out.

Marianne noticed what he was looking at and asked him whether he was worried about his horse. He told her about the plastic pails and the soccer ball, about the candy wrappers, and about how Loki picked pockets.

"Loki has nothing to do all day long," Matt told her. "He's bored."

Marianne thought for a moment. "Some horses have hard balls to knock around their stalls, balls that can take a real beating. You could probably find one at the discount supermarket for pets, the new one in the mall that's been advertising special low prices."

"It has stuff for horses?" Matt asked.

"Those balls are sold for dogs, too," she told him. "You'll want to get the biggest size."

"He won't break it?"

"I think those balls are indestructible," she said, "but they're not cheap. So try the discount store."

Matt told Linda and Alan about Loki's boredom. He

told them Marianne had practically ordered him to get that special ball. Linda was willing to help with the money, but Alan frowned and shook his head.

"It costs and costs," he complained. "Even if the horse farm finds a customer that'll pay a bundle for him and we all get back what we've put out, there's other things I'd like to do with my money right now. Besides," he added, "if Loki's as valuable as Leroy says, when he's sold, we'll be so rich we can do anything we want. You can get riding lessons without all that work cleaning out the stall."

"I don't want riding lessons," Matt retorted, although that wasn't true.

Linda flew at Alan, accusing him of betraying Loki and of being selfish and lazy. "If you're counting on a payoff," she charged, "you can forget about it. Even if they sell Loki, you won't deserve anything, not if you turn your back on him now."

"I'm not turning my back on him," Alan told her. "I'm just being practical. If Mom and Dad decide to sell him, we're not going to be able to stop them. So we might as well cut our losses. Or," he added, "cash in on the sale."

"If you're the brains of this operation," she retorted, "how about using them to stop Mom and Dad from selling him?"

Alan glared at her, but he didn't reply. Linda glared back.

After a moment he opened his desk drawer. When he turned around, he was holding a ten-dollar bill, which he handed over to Matt. "I hope this doesn't lead to a life of crime," he muttered.

"What do you mean?" Matt asked as he pocketed the money.

"This horse thing," Alan told him. "It's an expensive habit. When people can't support their habits, they turn to crime."

Matt wasn't sure whether Alan was still ticked off or trying to be funny. He guessed it would be better not to ask. After all, Alan had just helped him afford the ball. That meant he hadn't given up on the horse entirely.

It was hard, though. Just as Matt had to remember to care about emus so that Leroy would care about Loki, now he had to be wary about Alan, who seemed to be running short of money and patience. Matt had no idea how to go about sparking Alan's interest again. All he knew was that he couldn't risk losing Alan to the other side.

23 | ALAN, WHO WAS old enough to go to the mall with his friends, refused to be seen in a pet store, even a super one. So Matt had to bide his time until Mom and Dad announced a major shopping trip. When Matt said he and Linda and Jerry needed to go to the super pet store, Mom supposed it was to check out dog items.

"Look at pictures of different breeds," she called as they ran toward the enormous store at the far end of the parking lot.

"Stay together," Dad reminded them.

Inside they found aisle after aisle of shelves packed with rubber toys and rawhide bones and catnip mice. There were doggy sweaters and raincoats, bottles of smells to get rid of smells, beds and pads and cushions, gates and cages and crates, bags and cans of dog and cat food, and an entire wall hung with collars and leashes of every size and color.

It was Linda who found Loki's new stall toy. It was bright red, heavy and hard, and the size of a basketball. It also cost more than they had expected. They seemed to be a dollar short.

Still, they brought the ball with them to the checkout counter. A man waiting in line ahead of them said he had a ball like that and his dog was crazy about it. The three kids looked at one another.

"You go borrow some money," Linda told Matt. "Mom will think it's for your dog."

"I don't have a dog," Matt replied. "Jerry can go. They wouldn't not lend him a dollar."

Jerry said, "We're supposed to stay together. They'd get mad if I went by myself."

By now they were at the register. The checkout woman told them what they owed. They had enough.

But Matt said, "Are you sure? We added up and thought it was a dollar more."

"You're in luck," said the woman. "This is the last day of our grand opening month. That makes you members. Ten percent off everything."

Luck for Loki all over again, thought Matt, as the woman handed over some change and took down his name and address for the store's membership list.

"You should never give out your address," Dad said afterward. "That list is for advertising. We're doomed to one more weekly flyer with specials we don't need."

Jerry said, "But Matt got to be a member and paid less on account of it, and that goes for next time, too. My grandmother says anyone who misses a bargain deserves to pay through the nose."

"Well," admitted Dad grudgingly, "your grandmother is the champion of all bargain hunters. I guess we can put up with a little doggy junk mail."

The kids grinned at one another. It hadn't dawned on either parent that Matt had been shopping for his horse.

As soon as they got home, they went straight to the barn. At first Loki just eyed the ball. When Matt rolled it toward him, Loki stepped out of its way.

"Man," said Jerry, "and that was a pretty expensive bargain. What if he won't play with it?"

Matt just shook his head. He hoped Alan didn't get wind of this failure.

But that evening when Matt went out to feed and water Loki, there was a pounding in the barn that sounded like someone hammering and then dropping a hard, heavy object. Matt ran inside. Loki was knocking the ball from one side of the stall to the other. Matt approached quietly. He wished he could see over the door. He could only guess at the kind of footwork involved as Loki pivoted to slam the ball each time it bounced off the wall.

As the days went by, Loki invented new games with the ball. Since playing with it used up some of his energy and made him easier to handle outdoors, Matt and Jerry

and Linda began to give Loki's loyal fans brief rides. They had to promise not to tell anyone, but of course word was bound to get out. After all, there were always other kids on the ball field.

"You should charge those kids," Alan said after another trip to the riding stable for hay and bedding, which cost more than what Matt and Jerry had made from wheeling the garden cart around the neighborhood to deliver manure for people's gardens. "Do you know how much they'd have to pay to ride at the stable?"

"But they're our friends," Matt protested. "They're Loki's friends."

"Well," Alan retorted, "don't expect me to keep coughing up ten-dollar bills. At least cut down on your expenses. No more frills."

"What are frills?" Matt asked.

"That ball, for instance," Alan said.

"But Loki plays with it all day. It makes him happy."

Alan shrugged. "You know it's a losing battle."

Matt said, "I'm going to pay for everything. I just need to figure out how."

Alan shrugged again. But he sent Matt a long, considering look. "I guess you mean that, too. I guess we're all stuck with your gift horse."

Matt grinned.

But the good feeling didn't last long. As soon as Mom and Dad came home and opened the mail, Mom exclaimed over a letter from the horse farm that had shipped Loki to Marbury. Someone interested in Fjord horses might be calling and coming to see Loki in the next week or two.

Matt's heart sank.

"Look at it this way," Mom told him. "Once the horse thing is settled, we can look for a dog. Even a big dog if you want."

Matt opened his mouth. He didn't care what he said. He just felt like making a lot of noise.

But Alan didn't give him a chance. "Excellent!" he declared. "That ball's made for a big dog." As he spoke, he sent Matt a warning look

Dad pulled a sheet of paper out of another envelope. "Here," he declared, waving it at Matt. "Start planning. You might win a year's supply of food for your pet."

All three kids drew together to read about the pet show sponsored by the new pet supermarket, the humane society, and the trustees of Wilmot Place.

"I was joking," Dad told them as he started down the hall. "That was not a serious suggestion," he called back to them.

But they took the announcement and rules into Matt's room.

"It might not mean horses," warned Alan.

"It says any kind of pet," Linda pointed out. "Besides, there's a class for the most unusual one."

"We could ask," Matt said.

Alan shook his head. "Bad move. Don't give them a chance to say no."

"If Loki is the only horse," Linda declared, "he's got to win the unusual class."

"Unless someone enters an even more unusual animal," Matt said.

"Like what?" Linda asked.

"Like an emu," Matt replied.

They thought this over.

"Anyway," Alan told them, "even if Loki wins the most unusual pet category, he still has to be the best of the whole show to get a year's supply of food."

They trooped out to the barn to consider what other classes Loki ought to enter. Linda suggested the costume and disguise class. She could be a circus rider and do a few gymnastic stunts on his back while Matt kept Loki circling as if he were in a ring. They could decorate Loki's bridle and give him a plume for his head.

They looked at the announcement and rules again. Children had to have signed permission slips and health certificates for their pets. They had to be prompt and had to clean up after their pets. Then there was a lot of small print about dangerous animals being prohibited and the committee's right to request that an adult be present if there was any question about a child's ability to control his or her pet.

"We've got the health papers," Matt declared. "They came with Loki."

"I'm not sure Mom and Dad will sign a permission slip," Alan said. "They're too worried that there'll be complaints about the horse being here."

"We'll get Leroy," Matt declared. And then it occurred to him that if they made Loki a circus pony, that would leave Jerry out. They had to think of something else.

Linda said, "His mane's getting long. We might need to trim it."

Loki's stand-up mane had grown and was beginning to flop sideways. "It's supposed to be like a zebra's mane," Matt declared. And then, as he gazed at his beloved horse, it suddenly came to him how to make sure that Loki was the most unusual pet in the show. "He can be a zebra!" he declared. "He's already got leg stripes. We can paint the rest to match. That way he can be entered for best disguise as well as most unusual and friendliest. He might win all three."

But there was a problem. The show was three weeks off. The person interested in Fjord horses could show up any day. Somehow they had to stall for time. That meant getting their parents to go along with at least some of their plan. "You see?" Alan reminded Matt. "That's why you can't afford to get mad."

"All I want is to save Loki," Matt answered.

By the time Dad called them to supper, they were busy figuring out whether they could really pull it off.

24 | "FOLLOW MY LEAD," whispered Alan on the way into the dining room.

Mom and Dad were talking about work, but Mom gave Matt an especially loving smile. She was grateful to him for not making a fuss over the visitor who might soon come and take the horse off their hands. She went right on talking about some tour sponsor who was giving their travel agency a hard time.

There was lasagna for supper, Matt's favorite. He dug in.

Alan waited for the discussion to wind down. Matt glanced across the table at him, and Alan met his look with a slight nod. It was like a signal in a spy movie.

Poor parents, thought Matt. They never suspected that Alan was setting them up.

When Alan finally spoke, he used a tone that reassures grown-ups, especially parents. Thoughtfully, quietly, he mentioned what bugged him about selling Loki right now. Not that he cared much one way or another about horses. Still, he could see that the whole neighborhood had come to enjoy Loki. People would miss him when he was gone.

Alan paused to let this view sink in. Then he went on. "In a way it's brought us closer. We're more of a community. So I was thinking we maybe ought to do something, you know, like thank everyone for being so interested in the horse and not complaining. Like we could give a sort of farewell party and invite everyone to come and like maybe get their kids' pictures taken sitting on Loki. Then they'd have something to remember him with, something to treasure."

Treasure! Matt's mouth fell open. He forgot to eat. How did Alan think up words that parents always fell for?

He even told them that if they made it a family occasion, there would be plenty of adults to share the responsibility of holding small kids on Loki's broad, safe back. "Right?" he asked Linda and Matt.

"Right," Linda promptly agreed. "We'll put up signs all around like they do for lost cats."

"We could do it at the lot next to the baseball—" Matt added.

"We could," Alan interrupted, signaling Matt to keep his mouth shut, "but we know you wouldn't want to hang out there all day long on a spring weekend. Besides, those special pictures will deserve a decent background."

"So where—" Mom started to ask.

"Behind the barn," Linda suggested. "The ground's good and hard now, so Loki won't make holes, and the flowers—those flowers . . ." Her eyes went to Alan, then to Matt, who couldn't guess what she was appealing for but figured he could help out with this line of thought.

"The daffodils would be nice behind Loki," he said.

"Yes, the daffodils," Linda said with relief.

"And the early tulips are about to open," Mom chimed in, hooked.

At last the children could sit back and give their parents a chance to talk. Matt was amazed at how smoothly they progressed from tulips to dates and times. Maybe weekend after next, they said.

Matt flashed a questioning look at Alan. Wasn't that the pet show weekend?

Alan shook his head.

"Besides," Linda was saying, "even if those people decide to take Loki, can't they wait a week or so? It's bad enough that he has to go. Think how Matt feels."

Matt felt their eyes on him. He put his forkful of lasagna back on the plate. The full import of his loss wouldn't show, not after the way he had been feeding his face. All he could do was act brave and let them see how he was sparing them his pain.

Both parents melted. Dad said he would bake cupcakes for Loki's farewell party. Mom said she would provide some props like a cowboy hat or a fancy shirt for kids to wear to get their pictures taken.

"There ought to be a charge for those things," Alan said.

"Charge?" demanded Dad. "I thought this was to promote goodwill in the neighborhood."

"It was. It is. Still, people may want to help with the high cost of keeping Loki."

"But that's just the point," Mom objected. "We're not keeping him. That's what this is all about."

"Only we can't be sure when he's going," Linda reminded her. "We have to keep feeding him as long as he's here."

"And he needs new shoes," Matt blurted.

"New shoes!" Mom exclaimed. "Is he growing?"

"No," Matt told her, "but his feet are."

Dad groaned. "It's like having another kid. Thank goodness we don't have to worry about sending him to college."

By the end of dinner it was agreed that a basket might be provided for those who felt like donating something to help with the hay and a blacksmith.

And, Matt figured as he lay in bed that night, if the basket filled up with dollar bills, and if Loki went on to win a year's supply of food, maybe Mom and Dad would change their minds about sending him away. At least they might consider using the money to board him at the stable outside town.

It seemed to Matt that even if he couldn't see Loki every day and take care of him, if he went somewhere not too far where there was room for him to get out and kick up his heels, it would make all the difference. Then instead of feeling as though he were sending Loki away, Matt would feel as though he were letting him go almost free.

25] "IF YOU'D MENTIONED the pet show, you would've blown it," Alan told Matt the next morning. "They don't have a clue. Never give parents something to say no about."

"Why would they say no about the pet show?" Matt asked.

Alan shook his head. "Don't you know parents like to say no after they've said yes? It's to show they're still in control."

"But the pet show was Dad's idea."

"It was Dad's idea of a joke," Alan reminded him.

Still, Matt wished he could talk to Mom and Dad about his plans. He needed to find out what kind of paint he should use to make Loki's zebra stripes.

He asked Leroy, who wasn't too keen about the idea. It might not be safe. Paint could act like poison. Leroy wondered what Matt's parents thought about it.

"They don't know yet," Matt told him.

"We're going to surprise them," Jerry added.

His dad looked thoughtful. "They're not big on surprises," he remarked. "Especially horse surprises."

Matt told Leroy all about the picture-taking session planned for a week from Sunday. It showed that Mom and Dad had a new atttude about Loki. "Anyway," Matt remembered to say, "the pet show was Dad's idea in the first place. Sort of as a joke. Only the zebra part came after. Can you find out if there's a paint that won't hurt Loki?"

Jerry's father said he would look into it. He also said he thought the zebra disguise was clever since Loki already had something of a zebra look. Matt felt better.

News of the farewell party swept through school before the notices went up around the neighborhood. Loyal Loki fans offered to help, and countless other kids saw the photo session as an excuse to haul out last fall's Halloween costumes and fool around all over again.

At home Mom and Dad and Jerry's family all pitched in. Serena put herself in charge of the dress-up box. Both mothers helped Linda with the signs that would direct people toward costumes, the horse, and refreshments (free, but with a donation basket front and center on the table).

On Saturday stakes were set up, and areas roped off. Each person who checked out the scene moved the stakes and connecting twine to improve the traffic flow. Pretty soon the lawn looked like green Swiss cheese, but Matt's mother didn't even frown at all the holes.

Mom's being that nice about the lawn made Matt uneasy. Maybe she was keeping some bad news from him. "Did those people say when they're coming to see Loki yet?" he asked.

Mom looked up from the flower bed, one hand full of twigs and dead weeds. "They weren't sure. I told them anytime since the horse is always here."

"Unless we take him over to the lot," Matt pointed out.

"Yes, but you're never gone for long. And we know where to find you."

Matt said nothing.

Mom stood up. "I know it's on your mind. You mustn't worry. We're going to be looking these people over while they're looking over the horse. We won't send him away with just anyone."

It was on the tip of Matt's tongue to beg her to postpone the visit. If Loki won the grand prize at the pet show, he would have a year's supply of food. And how could zebra Loki fail to win?

Jerry and Matt lugged pails of warm water from the house to wash Loki, but they had to rinse him with the hose. He didn't seem to mind the cold water. Like Missy in the bathtub slapping the surface and chasing suds, he played with everything he could reach. Wrinkling his nose and sneezing, he tried to stop the stream pouring out of the hose nozzle. While Matt snaked the water in front of him, Loki whipped his head from side to side, pounced, and seized the end of the hose in his teeth. For one instant the flow was blocked. Then the hose jumped and the water spurted all over the boys. Loki shook himself in triumph.

By noon on Saturday the area in front of the barn looked as though it had been hit by a flash flood. But the sun shone and repaired the worst of it, and the signs helped to draw people around to the back. Alan, who took on the role of police chief, assigned every Loki fan a position. In case of trouble they were to report to him.

"And you will report to your mother or me," Dad told him.

"If I can't handle it," Alan said.

"We're counting on you," Mom declared.

Jerry's father raised his eyebrows. "On Alan?"

Jerry's mother said, "Leroy!" in a warning tone.

Serena, fixing Linda with a look, asked who was going to mind Missy.

Linda said, "I'm helping with the horse."

"This is as much kids as horse," Mom reminded her, but Linda had already latched on to Loki.

"How about a photo of Jerry and Missy on Loki?" Leroy suggested.

Everybody agreed that this was a good way to begin.

Matt told Linda he didn't need any help holding Loki, but she refused to let go of the lead rope. Matt felt like yanking it out of her hand, but he was afraid it would start a fight and ruin everything. Anyway, he didn't want to upset Loki, who looked almost white in the bright sun, his thick forelock and tail fluffed out and gleaming, picture perfect.

Jerry stepped on the upside-down tub and mounted Loki. Leroy handed Missy up to him and then went behind the horse in case Missy squirmed out of Jerry's grasp.

"You're in the picture," Trish complained.

"Tough," Leroy retorted. "This is our daughter, not a doll. I'm staying right here."

Trish snapped a picture. She said, "Jerry, smile," and snapped another.

Jerry's grip tightened. "I think Missy's slipping," he said.

Missy started to whimper. Arching her back, she tried to fling herself free.

"Missy, smile," he commanded. "Shut up and smile."

"You're squeezing her," Leroy told him.

Trish snapped another picture, even though Missy was wailing and wouldn't smile.

"If all the picture taking goes like this," Dad said, "we'll be here till next week."

As soon as Leroy rescued Missy, Jerry slid from the horse. "She spoiled it," he muttered to Matt. "She always does."

So Matt let Jerry hold Loki for the next few pictures, the real ones with kids in party dresses and cowboy hats and boots with fake spurs, most of these kids proudly grinning and waving to the cameras.

26 | NOT ALL THE children were small or in costume. Matt noted that almost as many boys as girls from his grade showed up. Most of them said they just came to check out the scene and then stayed long enough to hike themselves onto Loki's back. They claimed they didn't care about pictures, but Matt's father was ready with plenty of film.

They all wanted to ride with no one holding on to the halter rope. Matt's father started to explain about safety and rules until Leroy took over and worked out a plan that allowed each one a quick turn around the backyard. After that they had to make room for the younger kids.

Through all this Loki showed his best manners. It seemed as though nothing could set him off until a mother, decked out in a flowery dress and a broad-brimmed straw hat, decided to be in the picture with her two small children. She handed her camera to Matt's dad and took her place at Loki's shoulder so that she faced the little ones perched on his back. Then she smiled to prompt smiles from them.

Dad focused the camera. "Ready?" he asked.

Still smiling, she nodded. It was more than Loki could resist. Without taking a step, without unsettling his two riders, he bent his neck as if to look around at them and chomped on the straw brim of the mother's hat. Everyone could hear the crunch.

Linda sprang forward to grab Loki's head. Matt, who had tried to stay out of the picture by giving Loki some free rein, yanked him straight. But it was too late.

The mother covered the bitten part of the brim as if it were a wound. Dad announced on a note of triumph that he had recorded the deed on film. Mom sidled up to him and whispered something that made him look and sound sorry about the hat. To make the mother feel better, he took many more pictures. He assured her that the bite out of the hat would not be visible.

Meanwhile Loki, wearing his look of wide-eyed innocence, munched and munched and then spit out the chewed straw. Matt kicked the mess into the flower bed.

Once the shock wore off, the mother decided to be

a good sport about the whole thing. Linda directed her and her much-photographed children to the refreshment table, where Trish plied them with cupcakes, one for each hand.

"You have to be careful," Dad told Matt.

There wasn't time for a more serious scolding. People kept coming, some with video cameras to shoot brief rides, but most hoping to get a photo they could frame. When Loki snorted at one boy dressed as Big Bird, Linda convinced the kid that Big Bird didn't ride horses and then asked him if he would like to be a pirate instead. She helped Serena put together a pirate outfit for the little boy and then started to dress up others. The costumes got all mixed up. Some kids wore military jackets and feather headdresses; some wore clown shirts and cowboy hats; some wore Batman capes with knights' helmets.

As everyone traded finery, the lines began to jam up. Kids had to go out of turn in order to make use of this or that special prop or costume. There were a surprising number of girls in real black velvet riding hats. These got passed up and down the line. Naturally the owners of the riding hats had to hang around and wait to get them back.

Alan kept everyone in strict line until Leroy told him

to lighten up. He would do better to explain the setup to the new arrivals, who were so far back that they couldn't even see the horse.

After Alan went off to talk to the people still waiting down the driveway, Linda reappeared for a turn holding Loki. Matt and Jerry took off for a pail of water. On their way they caught sight of Alan and an irate woman who was complaining in a loud voice that she hadn't come all this way to stand around. She demanded to see Mr. or Mrs. Hoffman.

Matt and Jerry took one look at her and her child, a girl dressed from head to toe in a perfect riding outfit, before they scooted into the barn. When they came out again with the water, the woman was still giving Alan a hard time, but now some of the other waiting parents were coming to his defense.

"The Hoffmans have their hands full," declared Chris Mascarello's father, who had already been through the line once and was back with two more children. "Everyone has to wait their turn. Everyone!" he explained as he looked the woman up and down.

Matt could see that the woman thought she and her daughter had special rights. Clearly Mr. Mascarello didn't agree.

"I came to see the horse," she argued.

"So did I," declared another waiting mother.

"So did they all," Alan said. "And up to now everyone has been patient and nice."

"I don't care about nice," the woman fumed.

"Obviously," remarked Mr. Mascarello.

Matt ran to Alan. "Shall I get Dad?" he asked.

"Yes!" answered the woman.

"No," said Alan in what was nearly a shout.

"We're doing fine," Mr. Mascarello told Matt. "Your dad's got plenty on his hands without having to put up with one bad attitude."

"Attitude?" the woman retorted.

"Go on," Alan muttered to Matt. "Keep Dad and Mom busy back there."

"But Dad said if there was a problem—"

"I'm handling it," Alan snapped. His voice dropped to a whisper. "She's here for Loki. At least I think she is. Go on now. Get lost."

Matt turned back to Jerry. Together they carried the water around to Loki, who was thirsty just from standing around all afternoon and having his picture taken.

"Everything all right out front?" Dad asked Matt. "Does Alan need some backup?"

Loki, blowing bubbles in the bottom of the pail, raised his head and let water dribble out of his mouth. Matt, who was used to Loki's drinking games, stepped nimbly out of the way. Everyone watching laughed. No bad attitudes here, thought Matt.

And then it struck him. Alan thought the woman with the attitude and the kid in fancy riding clothes were here to look over Loki, to see about buying him.

Matt laughed with the others who were laughing at Loki. Holding the horse's head firmly as the next parent in line hoisted a child onto Loki's back, he turned to answer his father's question. "Alan's doing great," he said.

Another child was seated on Loki. As the father stepped aside and aimed the camera, a Loki fan came running into the backyard. Pausing to keep from crossing in front of the camera until the picture was taken, she dashed up to Matt to report trouble out front. But before she could finish, the woman who had tangled with Alan marched past everyone waiting in line. The other parents broke ranks to block her. Everyone had to take turns, they tried to explain. It wasn't fair to barge in front of kids who had been in line for more than an hour.

"Where is Mrs. Hoffman?" the woman demanded.

"Gone for doughnuts," someone said. "They ran out of cupcakes."

"This is impossible. Where is Mr. Hoffman?"

But Dad had heard enough. He helped the next child onto Loki and then started toward the cluster of parents and the insistent mother in their midst.

Matt froze. Was Loki doomed?

Still walking toward her, Dad began to speak in a polite but firm voice. "Excuse me," he said. "It'll be a shame if one person ruins our neighborhood event. Everyone is welcome. But this is a private home, and I'm going to have to ask you to take your place in line and show the same courtesy and good humor that everybody else has done, or else leave."

Oh, yes, please, willed Matt, his thoughts echoing Alan's words: Go on. Get lost.

Wheeling, the woman collided with Matt's mother, who happened to arrive, laden with boxes of doughnuts, at the very instant the woman flung herself away. All the grown-ups grabbed the cartons that went flying out of Mom's arms.

"What was that all about?" she exclaimed as people carried the saved doughnuts to the refreshment table, everyone talking at once and laughing again.

"That person was not a happy camper," said Trish, "and she didn't even get her hat eaten."

Dad came alongside Mom and put his arm around her shoulders. "Nothing to speak of," Matt heard him say. "Just one bad apple. I doubt she'll hang around."

Matt heaved a sigh of relief. Then it was time to move Loki out of the late-afternoon sun so that the light would be just right for the remaining people who had been so patient and helpful.

Matt could see that Loki was getting bored and restless. "It's almost over," Matt whispered to him. Loki lowered his head and rubbed it against Matt's shirt. Matt told him to stand. With one hand gripping the reins, he parted the black and white forelock, scrubbed with his fingers up and down the horse's face, and gazed with love into the dark, wide-set eyes.

27 | "STRANGE THAT THOSE people never came to see the horse," Mom said. It was Wednesday, a school half day, and she had come home from work at noon to organize the cleanup from Sunday's event.

Matt's and Linda's eyes met, and then each bent to the task at hand.

But Mom noticed. "Did they call again?" she asked. "The woman seemed so interested when we spoke on the phone."

Matt dragged the trash bag to the bin. "Not that I

know of," he answered. He could feel his ears go hot. They were bound to give him away. "Honestly," he added. He glanced at Linda. She was raking the torn-up part of the lawn.

"Maybe they changed their mind," she said. "Anyway"—she went on—"it gives us time to get Loki ready for the pet show."

"Um," said Mom, clipping broken stems and staking the peonies. Alan had been right about waiting to mention it. By Sunday night both parents were so mellow about the horse that they saw no reason to object to his going to the show.

Before long two Loki fans showed up to help. They even brought a mother to lend a hand. The mother, who provided a bag of grass seed, told Matt's mom how much everyone appreciated what the Hoffmans had done for the neighborhood.

Leroy and Jerry were late because they were hunting down all the black finger paint in Marbury. Finger paint, Leroy had decided, was the only really safe paint for Loki's zebra stripes.

Long before Alan got home from soccer practice, everything was pretty well put to rights. Mom said the kids could take Loki out to the vacant lot until supper time.

"She'll find out," Matt said to Linda as they led the

horse down Plympton Street with Jerry on his back.

"It doesn't matter," Linda replied. "That woman didn't call, so we didn't lie. Forget about it."

"I can't," he whispered. "They're going to be so mad."

Linda shrugged. "Not at us. Dad was the one that told her off." She giggled. "Wasn't it great?"

But Matt was too worried to take pleasure in the memory of the showdown between Dad and the awful woman who had come to see Loki. Was this what getting even was all about? Why didn't it feel good?

At least he could still enjoy the horse. When it was Matt's turn to ride, he tried a new trick, swiveling around so that he was riding backward. Linda dared him to stand up on Loki's back like a circus rider, but it was easier said than done. Loki's broad, rounded back looked so solid until Matt tried to straighten his legs and stand tall. Then nothing stayed firm. It took only a shake of Loki's head to unbalance Matt.

The Loki fans, who had tagged along, wanted to try. But Linda got sensible and bossy, reminding them that if one kid got hurt, the parents might put an end to their fun. "Let's get through next weekend," she said. "Then if Loki wins big, we'll be able to do whatever we want. Next year he can be a circus horse for the show and we'll all get to stand on his back."

She sounded so sure that Loki would still be with them. But Matt couldn't think beyond the next few days.

On the way home they discussed how and when to start painting the stripes. They decided to experiment with the finger paint the next afternoon.

"Don't use too much," Jerry warned. "My father says we probably ought to have more, but he bought all there was."

"Don't forget to pay him back," Linda said to Matt.

Matt nodded. There was so much to think about, so much to do. It was a relief just to give Loki his hay, to rinse out the pail and fill it before carrying it into the stall.

Matt stayed a moment longer, just to watch Loki as he fed. The horse had a habit of shifting his weight from one front foot to the other, as if part of him were still on the move while the feeding part of him dug into the hay. Did he remember how he used to be let out into a field of grass where he could wander at will? Matt went close to him and leaned against one foreleg. He pressed his face against Loki's shoulder and felt the muscle twitch under the warm skin.

28 | THE FINGER PAINT looked fine as it went on, but as soon as it dried, it began to flake off. Matt asked Jerry to speak to his dad about it. On Friday afternoon Leroy showed up with paintbrushes, buckets, bottles, soap, and mild detergent. Matt and Jerry and Linda stood by, handing him whatever he asked for.

Alan, who stopped in to see what they were up to, said they looked like doctors in a TV hospital show. He also said that the stripes didn't look like zebra stripes.

"I'm not the artist here," Leroy told him. "I'm the technical consultant."

"You need zebra pictures to copy," Alan pointed out.

Leroy straightened, dropped a rag into a bucket of suds, and sent Alan a hard look. "Are you here to harass, hinder, or help?" he asked.

Alan shrugged.

"Why don't you make yourself useful and go to my house and pick out a few books with zebra illustrations? Look for African animals on the third shelf up behind my desk."

Alan nodded and was gone. Leroy turned to the others. "Here's the deal. You need to add some of this cornstarch to the paint. Then if you wipe Loki's coat with warm water and vinegar, with just a touch of detergent, you'll get rid of enough surface oil so that the paint will hold. But easy on the detergent or you'll irritate his skin."

"What about the vinegar?" asked Linda. "Won't it sting?"

"Feel it," he answered, pointing to the bucket. "If it doesn't bother you, it won't bother the horse."

All three kids stuck their hands in the water mixture.

"You'll do best with a sponge," Leroy told them. "And use really good towels to wipe off the excess water before you paint. Do just a small area at a time. Okay?"

They nodded. Matt wished Leroy would stay and oversee their painting. But Leroy said it was their project, not his. He had other things to do.

Alan returned with three books, each with photographs of zebras. Linda gazed at a zebra face head-on. That's where they would have to start, with Loki's face.

But he didn't want to hold still. He kept thrusting his muzzle, trying to nibble on the paintbrush.

"I'll get carrots," Matt said. "That'll keep him still."

"And towels," Linda called after him as she started to sponge off Loki's face.

Matt raced around the house, collecting guest towels

from the linen closet and carrots from the refrigerator. And marshmallows. Loki loved marshmallows more than anything else.

"Those fancy towels got wet too quickly. Try bath towels," Linda instructed him.

"Leroy said good towels," Matt reminded her. "Really good."

"Look." She showed him how quickly the guest towels soaked up water. "We need big ones."

Matt ran back and gathered every towel hanging in the bathroom.

Back in the barn, he bit off pieces of carrot to feed to Loki, who soon figured out when the next offering was coming from the sound of the carrot snapping.

"Stop it," Linda ordered. "Keep him still." With intense concentration she drew a diamond in the middle of Loki's forehead. It looked strange, like a decoration, until she followed it up with another diamond around the center one. Jerry practically hung from the halter to keep Loki's head low enough for Linda. Matt produced one marshmallow after another, pulling each one stealthily from the bag and then holding his hands under Loki's mouth so that the horse could keep on licking his fingers.

"There!" Linda finally declared, pulling back and gazing with pride on her work.

Jerry let go of the halter. Matt put aside the bag with its few remaining marshmallows. They stared and stared. The zebra effect was better than either of them had expected.

Matt took the next turn. Thickened with cornstarch, the paint tended to stiffen. The long stripes got jagged and uneven. At first that worried him. But when he had finished painting Loki's neck and was moving on down the withers to the upper foreleg with its real stripes, he checked the pictures again. The zebras in the books had crooked markings, too.

"My turn," Jerry declared. He grabbed the bucket and sloshed the water mixture onto the other side of Loki's neck.

"Careful!" Linda shouted. "You'll mess up his face." She and Matt blotted splashes that threatened the newly painted stripes.

"More towels," Jerry demanded. "He's too wet. Hurry."

Matt ran to the house for every remaining towel. The mound of sodden towels was growing by the minute. "Your house next," Matt said, biting off a tip of carrot.

Jerry shook his head. "My grandmother won't let us."

"Your dad will, though," Matt answered. "Tell Serena he told us to."

"Uh-huh," Jerry mumbled as he dipped into the paint. "Can you mix up some more? I'm almost out."

Matt hunted around until he found two more jars of black finger paint. "Someone better find out where the rest is," he said as he dumped in the cornstarch and then stirred the mixture with a stick.

"Too thick," Jerry pronounced after starting to paint with this new batch.

Matt and Linda went around to examine Jerry's side. They could see that the paint wouldn't flow. The stripes were thicker than Matt's.

"Add water," Linda directed.

But Matt was afraid the color would lighten. "We'd better ask Leroy."

Jerry kept on working while Matt went across the street to the Brewster house. But Serena said Leroy had had to go back to school for something. She had no idea when he would get home.

Matt went to look for Alan, who was busy with the computer and didn't want to stop. Eventually, with much groaning, he followed Matt out to the barn. Matt could tell that Alan was impressed with the zebra look.

He sort of whistled and shook his head. "Not bad," he declared. But when he went around to Jerry's side, he scowled. "The two sides don't match," he said.

"We know," Linda told him. "But no one sees both sides at the same time. The real problem is that we made the paint too thick. And I think we're running out."

Alan suggested thinning with water. "After all," he pointed out, "this isn't art. It's a disguise, a game." But he couldn't keep from adding, "Man, that face, though. You'd swear it was a zebra."

Alan hung around while Matt carefully stirred in more water. They all held their breaths as Jerry painted another stripe. At first it looked almost as black as the one before. But as it dried, it got lighter.

"What'll we do?" Matt said. "We're not even halfway done."

"Wait." Alan sorted through the books and picked up one they hadn't used. "Hold on," he said, riffling through the pages. "I saw something that might work."

They waited without speaking. Not one of them could imagine that there was a way out of this predicament.

"All right!" Alan announced. "Here's your answer, guys." He laughed as he held open the book. "Look at what I've got for you. Am I the brains, or what?"

Matt peered at the blurry black-and-white photograph on the page. He saw an animal that looked like half a zebra. About midway along the animal's body the stripes faded and then disappeared altogether. "What's that?" he asked.

"'A quagga,'" Alan read. "An extinct quagga."

"For real?" asked Jerry.

"But it's ugly," Linda exclaimed. "Loki's beautiful. So are zebras."

"Forget beautiful," Alan told her. "Start making signs to tell the world you've come up with the rarest animal of all, thought to be extinct. Loki here is the last surviving member of his species. From darkest . . . somewhere."

"Where?" asked Matt.

"Oh, I don't know. Make it up."

"But there really was a quagga once?"

"Read about it," Alan told him. "It'll give you ideas for your signs." He glanced again at Loki. "Don't stop painting, though. Finish those stripes. They should fade away just like in the picture." He looked down on the barn floor. "And clean up before Mom and Dad get home." He kicked at the pile of towels.

By the time Matt and Jerry and Linda had used up all the watered paint, they were able to convince themselves that Loki was a nearly perfect quagga. Matt wished they had saved a little paint in case he needed a touch-up tomorrow. He told Loki not to lie down and not to play with his water. Loki responded by stretching out his neck and curling his lip. Matt popped a marshmallow into his mouth. Loki nodded his head, up and down, up and down, as he sucked and slobbered his treat.

There wasn't a single clean towel left. Matt had to borrow some from Serena.

"Did your mother send you?" she asked.

"She's not home yet," he replied. "I know she needs some. I'm trying to help," he added.

Serena gave him a doubting look, but she heaped towels into his arms and let him out the door. He made it safely home before his parents' car pulled into the driveway.

29 | THEY NEARLY DIDN'T make it to the pet show. A phone call interrupting dinner Friday night brought the news that Matt had dreaded. It came not from the woman but from the distant farm that had put the possible buyer in touch with the Hoffmans.

According to the horse farm person, the buyer had come all the way to the Hoffmans' only to be ignored and then treated rudely.

"Everyone's mad at us," Mom declared, directing a searching look at each of her children.

"Do you suppose it was that—uh, the lady that knocked over the doughnuts?" Alan asked. "She looked pretty mad, but I didn't see what set her off."

Dad groaned. "Oh, no. The one who barged through the line?"

Alan shrugged, managing a look of unconcern. "Could be."

Matt didn't say a word. He knew he could never sound that cool.

"Didn't she tell anyone who she was?" Dad demanded.

Matt copied Alan's shrug. Linda shook her head.

"The woman you told off?" Mom said to Dad.

They started arguing, Mom insisting that Dad call the woman and apologize and Dad maintaining that he had been doing his best to keep everyone happy, and it wasn't his fault. After a while he said he wouldn't apologize unless the woman did, and Mom accused him of being stubborn because he was wrong. And then the argument fizzled because both of them wanted to blame the kids and weren't sure they could.

It wasn't until later, when Mom discovered that every single towel had been used on Loki, that she lost her temper and told Matt that he was grounded for the weekend.

Linda leaped to his defense. "That's not fair," she said. "We both used them."

"Then you're both grounded," Mom retorted.

Linda went to help Dad with the dishes. While she was putting things away, she told him all about Loki's transformation and begged Dad to come see the signs she had painted to educate the public about animals that really become extinct.

Dad, who had calmed down by now, was impressed by the signs and even more impressed when Linda took him out to see Loki. He came back into the house full of ideas for improving the disguise. With Leroy's book open to the quagga picture, he pointed out that Loki's tail and forelock were too thick and long.

When he tried to convince Matt that they should cut Loki's tail and forelock, Mom was pulled into the debate, too. Dad showed her the picture and took her out to see the painted horse. Then he asked for her opinion. She told him it didn't matter since she had just grounded Matt and Linda for the weekend.

"You could defer the grounding," he said.

"You could apologize to that woman," she replied.

They went into their room and shut the door.

"Quick," Alan commanded. "Get the towels in the washing machine. You were supposed to do that hours ago."

"I was going to," Matt said. "But Linda told me she would because I do it wrong."

"I forgot," Linda told them. "We got started on the signs and I forgot."

By the time their parents emerged, the first load of towels was in the dryer and the second load was being washed. Somehow things looked less overwhelming. Mom and Dad didn't say what had been decided about the angry woman, but they did tell Matt and Linda that they could take their grounding the following weekend.

"It'll be hard on Loki," Matt said. "He'll miss his exercise."

"Don't push your luck," Mom told him. "That's the deal. Take it or leave it."

Matt and Linda said they would take it. And then everyone had to figure out how much time it would take for Loki to walk to Wilmot Place. It was finally decided that they would go in a convoy with one car in front and one behind. Leroy was consulted about a safe route. He volunteered to lead the way.

All that remained to be dealt with was Loki's tail and

forelock. Matt finally gave in about the tail, but he so loved the way Loki's forelock looked that he couldn't bear the idea of cutting it.

Jerry, who had come over with his dad to help get everything set for the morning, stopped Linda just as she was about to trim the thick tail. "You could wrap it in tape to make it skinny. The same up front."

He helped her press Loki's tail hair down while Matt tore off strips of black electrical tape to bind it. When Linda was finished, Loki looked even more like the picture than before.

It was harder "up front," as Jerry called it, because Loki wouldn't hold still. Both boys had to stuff marshmallows into his mouth to give Linda time to reduce Loki's ample forelock to a mere brush.

"He looks fine," Mom declared when everyone came out to inspect. "You've done a terrific job, all of you." She beamed at her family as though nothing had gone wrong. She sounded as though she really meant it, too. She was proud of them.

Linda signaled to Matt. Now was a good time to get back to the laundry. They had a heap of towels to fold and sort before they went to bed.

30 | EARLY SATURDAY morning there were so few cars out that Leroy was able to lead the convoy right across the busiest intersection in town. Loki stopped what traffic there was.

"He's a quagga," Alan said to a truck driver, who slowed to make room for Alan on his bike. "Quaggas are like real, only extinct. Except this one's like, you know, a gag."

"Uh-huh," said the truck driver, staring in disbelief.

Last night Alan had printed out an information sheet about quaggas. He had said on it that quaggas were killed off in the last century because people didn't protect endangered species. Alan had gone on to list other animals facing the same fate today. He had checked this out with Leroy, who had told him to make lots of copies. So Alan had used up all the printer paper in his house.

As the truck rumbled past the convoy, the grown-ups darted looks of alarm. But the kids, who were used to walking Loki past noisy garbage trucks and chippers, knew Loki wouldn't freak. He seemed to enjoy this early-morning outing. He was like a tourist, looking every which way, not wanting to miss a thing.

It was only when they marched past the fire station

that Matt shortened the lead rope. But nothing happened. The fire engines stayed inside. A couple of firefighters stood in the doorway and waved.

On walked Loki, full of energy. But his escorts, Matt and Linda and Jerry, were puffing a bit. Each of them knew it was possible to hitch a ride in one of the cars, but no one wanted to admit to having trouble keeping up.

"How much farther?" Matt asked Jerry.

"How do I know?" Jerry replied.

"You ought to," Linda told him. "Your father goes there all the time."

"Not like this," Jerry retorted. And then he exclaimed, "Look! There are the gates! We're almost there!"

The entrance to Wilmot Place was jammed. Someone told Matt where to go to register. One of the people at the registering table looked Loki up and down and said doubtfully, "We didn't expect any ponies."

"Horse," Matt corrected.

"Quagga," Jerry reminded him.

"He's a pet," Linda declared, "and we came to enter him."

"Just a minute," said the registering person, going off to speak to a higher authority.

"Don't worry," said the next registering person at the table. "We've already entered a python and an iguana. She can't refuse you."

The kids exchanged glances of relief.

The registering person returned and told them to go to the woman in the green baseball cap who was standing at the fork in the path.

"But we haven't said what classes we want to be in," Matt protested.

"I'll come and register you in a few minutes. Right now we have to get the pony away from all these people before someone gets kicked or stepped on."

"He doesn't kick," Matt told her. "And we've just walked beside him for more than three miles without getting stepped on."

"Come on," said Linda, grabbing Loki's lead rope. "Honestly, Matt," she said as they went to look for the woman in the green baseball cap, "you've picked a crummy time to start asserting yourself."

The green baseball cap was on Marianne's head. She beckoned to them and led them briskly along a row of temporary pens where a few kids with large dogs were already settling in. She stopped at the last pen.

"I think you'll fit in here," she said. "If Loki gets restless, just take him out behind and let him crop the grass. That'll keep him happy." She glanced at her clipboard. "I have to get back. Is there anything you need?"

Matt shook his head. "Mom and Dad brought all our stuff."

"I'll tell them where you are," Marianne promised. "Oh," she added, "Loki looks fantastic. I hope the rain holds off."

They all glanced up at the gray clouds massing overhead.

"Still," she declared cheerfully, "this kind of weather is a lot easier on the animals than bright sun. Except for the reptiles," she added. "I may have to put them indoors."

"Maybe if it rains, she'll put us indoors, too," Matt said hopefully.

But Jerry didn't think so. "My dad said we can't be treated specially just because of his connection here."

The grown-ups arrived with the bucket, signs, a card table, Alan's information sheets, and a bag of snacks. Mom and Dad were going to have to divide their time between the pet show and the soccer field, where Alan would be playing. He was already on his way there.

Linda, who went to remind the registration person that they needed to sign up for classes, was told to register then and there. She came back to announce that Loki was entered in three classes: for the most unusual pet, the best costume or disguise, and the friendliest. She also reported that there were three judges: a Marbury town official, the chairman of the trustees of Wilmot Place, and the president of the state humane society.

A newspaper photographer stopped by to take a picture of Loki. "I'd better call him a zebra," she said. "Our readers won't know about quaggas."

"But that's the whole point," Matt insisted, shoving one of Alan's printouts at her.

In the pen next to them a girl with a huge Bernese mountain dog had given up trying get the photographer to spell her dog's breed name correctly. "Don't sweat it," she advised Matt and Jerry and Linda. "They'll print what they want, anyway."

The kids tried to display the signs so that everyone who came by would be able to read them. After climbing onto Loki's back, Matt didn't dare stand to his full height. He used masses of tape to hang the biggest sign from the light wooden frame that crossed the front of the pen. Every time a breeze stirred, the sign flipped up. The girl with the Bernese mountain dog said she had borrowed a staple gun from a guy with Siberian huskies. Linda went in search of him. She was gone a long time. When she returned, they were able to staple the smaller signs to the uprights. Droves of people were already gawking at the big pets along this row.

Some of them read all the blurbs on the signs out loud to each other. They seemed to think that Loki was a real quagga. But Matt could tell that most people suspected that the kids had invented the animal and its name.

Jerry kept handing out information sheets in the hope that a few people would get it all together. Maybe they would read about quaggas later on and understand.

"I told someone I'd take a kitten," Linda confided in Matt.

"When?" asked Matt. "Who?"

"Some girl. She's saving it for me. Do you think Mom and Dad will let me?"

But Mom and Dad were gone and might not be back for hours.

Matt didn't know what to say. How could their parents refuse Linda a kitten when they had already offered him a dog? Still, parents were funny about things like that. "Show them the kitten first," he advised. "Don't tell them right away that you already said you'd take it."

"Right," Linda said. "They'll see how cute it is." She

gave him a steady look. "You've changed, you know. You've grown more brains since Loki came."

Matt felt his ears go warm, but this time he wasn't worried about what they looked like. Everyone had changed, he felt like saying. But here were more people to talk to, to explain about quaggas and other extinct or nearly extinct animals. He faced the public to tell his tale.

"And what class is he entered in?" asked a woman in a trench coat.

Jerry told her the three classes.

The woman strolled back along the row of pens and then returned with two men in tow, one sort of old and one sort of young. They stood back to examine the big sign that dangled above Loki. Then the woman asked the kids to bring him out of the pen so that they could look at him more closely.

Jerry gave each of them an information sheet. He said he was nearly out, but since they showed so much interest, he figured they each deserved to have one.

Loki, who thought he was going somewhere new and better, lurched forward. The younger man lurched, too, out of Loki's way.

Matt spoke to Loki, and Linda spoke to the man. The woman in the trench coat stepped closer to show that she wasn't afraid. She even patted Loki's neck. He blew warm breath at her and tried to nuzzle her hand. But she pulled back then; probably she didn't want his smell on her trench coat.

The older man asked questions about the paint and Loki's natural coloring and his upright mane. Matt responded by proudly showing off Loki's real stripes. One question led to another until all three kids were talking at once about the horse and the zebra idea and how hard it was to find enough nontoxic paint and about how patiently Loki had stood to be made into a quagga and how many marshmallows it had taken. The three people were such good listeners that Matt went on to tell them about Fjord horses, which were used on farms in Norway and were probably descended from the horses the Vikings rode hundreds of years ago. Then the younger man asked just one question: "Where do you live?"

Matt supplied the answer and went on to tell the older man and the trench-coat woman how he took care of Loki and about the vacant lot where they went for exercise.

The younger man didn't say another word.

31 | THE SKY DARKENED. A voice on the public-address system announced that the pet show sponsors were concerned for the well-being of the pets and their exhibitors. Because of the threatening weather, only the finalists in each class would be called into the ring.

The girl with the Bernese mountain dog said she was glad. "Jupiter's already panting hard. He can tell when a storm's coming. He freaks out when he hears thunder. Probably most of the dogs here do."

"But how will they choose the finalists?" Matt asked her.

"They've been doing that," she told him. "The judges have been all over the place looking at the pets."

Matt's heart sank. "They were here and we didn't know it?"

"You talked to them. You talked to them like forever."

Matt tried to think back to all the people who had stopped to look at Loki and ask questions. What did judges look like? If only they wore black robes like judges in court.

The finalists for the cutest pet class were called by name and told to bring their pets to the roped-off ring behind the big house. Matt didn't have to listen to the names; Loki hadn't been entered in that class.

It took awhile for the finalists for the cutest pets to assemble and for the placings to be announced. The best tricks class came next. Meanwhile the breeze picked up. The big sign flapped so hard that one of its taped hinges tore. As it dropped down over the front of the pen, even Loki was startled. Matt decided to give him a brief walk in the grassy area behind the pens to calm him down.

Mom showed up with rain jackets for all three kids. They put them on just to stay warm. The girl with the Bernese mountain dog looked on a bit wistfully, so Mom shrugged off her coat, peeled off the sweater she was wearing under it, and loaned it to the girl.

All this dressing was under way when the friendliest pet class was announced. Both the Bernese mountain dog and Loki were finalists, so they went together to the ring. The mean registering person didn't want to let in more than one kid with any pet. Matt insisted that Linda and Jerry were part of his team, but the registering person stood firm. So Linda and Jerry had to wait outside the gate.

Kids and pets lined up in the center of the ring. The woman in the trench coat and the two men walked toward the finalists. It began to sink in that those three, who had asked so many questions, were the judges. Matt couldn't guess what kind of impression Loki had made on them. Buffeted by the wind, they looked pinched with cold and not too pleased to be out in the weather with all these pets.

The registering person strode into the ring. She carried a cardboard carton that she presented to the judges. The trench-coat lady took a cup of something hot from the carton and wrapped her hands around it. The men did the same, shaking their heads at whatever else was in the carton. The registering person stood by while the judges conferred.

Then they beckoned to a boy with a fluffy black dog with big ears and no tail. Trench Coat stooped down to the dog, which flopped over onto its back and pawed the air. Next the judges called the girl with the Bernese mountain dog. The older man spoke and slapped his knee, and the dog rose up on its hind legs and put its massive forepaws over the man's shoulders. He staggered backward but kept his balance, supported by the other judges. The dog licked his face and eyeglasses.

Again the judges conferred. Trench Coat returned her cup to the carton and helped herself to a powdered jelly doughnut. Then she led the other judges over to Loki. Holding the doughnut in one hand, she stroked Loki's face with the other. Matt was helpless to prevent what was coming.

Loki leaned toward the partly eaten doughnut, pushed

his muzzle under Trench Coat's hand, and deftly nib-
bled his way upward. Trench Coat let go, of course. Loki
gobbled this super marshmallow and tried to cozy up
to Trench Coat to lick her fingers. To distract Loki,
Matt offered his own fingers, but the horse wasn't fooled.
He knew where the sugar was. Yearning toward Trench
Coat, he strained to follow her as she turned toward a
girl with a cat. Matt hauled on the lead rope with all
his might. The audience laughed. Someone yelled that
there was such a thing as being too friendly.

All Matt wanted was for this show to be finished.
When his name was called, he didn't even know enough
to step forward with Loki to receive his sixth-place ribbon. Jerry had to call to him, and Linda had to shout
a loud "thank you" to prompt him.

"Don't go," the registering woman ordered as he
started to lead Loki out of the ring. "You're in the next
class, too."

But it had begun to rain. Parents were demanding
that all the placings be announced. Surely the judges
had already made up their minds.

The girl with the Bernese mountain dog, which had
earned the title of friendliest pet, wished Matt luck
and ran to look for her parents' car before the thunder
started.

Back in the ring, the pace picked up. Two contestants

were in tears because their pets' costumes were getting wet. By the time Loki was declared winner of the costume and disguise class, his stripes were weeping, too. Matt couldn't believe how quickly all that careful painting dissolved into black smears. As Loki's stripes vanished, so did the natural ones on his legs, so blackened they became a blur.

The last class, the one for unusual pets, was in shambles. The announcer kept on sounding cheerful, but everyone, including the judges, had had enough. Half the finalists didn't attend because their animals couldn't be out in the cold rain. Only Loki looked perfectly happy under the downpour. He kept shaking himself and pawing the ground.

When his second place was announced, Matt was told to remain in the ring so that his ribbon and the grand champion trophy could be awarded together. He could hear Jerry yell, "We won! We won!" and then realized that the lead rope had slipped from his grasp.

It was confusing. The announcer boomed out one set of directions while Trench Coat beckoned and the registering person shouted something else. Thunder rumbled, and the rain fell harder. Matt distinctly heard another voice, a man's voice, objecting to the judges' decision. "We never meant we'd feed a horse for an entire year," the voice intoned. "Well, do something about it. Change it. What do you mean you can't?"

Matt couldn't hear the response or the responses. Trench Coat shoved a plaque at him and told him to put it under his jacket. While he tugged and struggled with it, Loki wandered over to a mud puddle, pawed once, folded his knees, and with a groan of joy sank down into the middle of it. He rolled first one way and then the other until he was slathered with mud. When he finally stood up again and shook, he spattered everything and everyone within range, including the registering woman, who shrieked in dismay and tried to protect the sodden box of doughnuts.

Her shriek caught Loki's attention. Even as Matt ran to grab the muddied lead rope, Loki pressed toward the shrieker and her box. He had just nudged open the cardboard flap when Matt got to him. All Loki was able to do before Matt yanked the questing muzzle aside was snort. Powdered sugar flew up, spraying the registering person and Matt. Blinking through powdered sugar and rain, Matt tried to find his way out of the ring. He needed to escape before Loki made things worse.

But there was more trouble outside. Linda met Matt with the news that the younger judge, sounding grim, had demanded to speak with Mr. or Mrs. Hoffman about keeping a horse on Plympton Street. It turned out, said Linda, that this judge was like the town boss.

Matt wiped the mess from his eyes. Of course, he thought, that man Loki had scared. The one who had asked only one question.

"What did Mom and Dad tell him?"

"That it's temporary," Linda answered. "A temporary arrangement."

All Matt's hopes were washed away like Loki's stripes. Temporary, he thought, was all his gift horse had ever been. So what was the use of winning a year's supply of food? The plaque slid down and dropped at his feet.

Jerry dived to retrieve it. "I'll carry this," he said. "Your folks went to get Alan. My dad says we're going home in the van. You're supposed to put Loki out with the sheep. He can stay there tonight. It's through that gate by the barn."

"Is it safe?" Matt asked. "Will someone feed him?"

Marianne, coming to meet them, said, "I'll be here."

"What if he freaks out in the storm?" Matt asked, thinking of the Bernese mountain dog.

"Then I'll put him in the barn. Leave his halter on. He'll be fine."

Not that Loki looked about to freak out. The pasture wasn't large, but it was the first real space he had known in many weeks. He took off with a mighty buck and galloped to the far end. Then he ran along the fence, stopping briefly to snort at the three horned sheep before racing himself to the end again. Nothing cramped his glee, nothing muted the beauty of him, neither rain nor thunder nor mud nor the last traces of black paint and sugar.

It was just as Matt had always imagined it would be when he set Loki free.

32

Dear Uncle Oliver:

How are you? How is the Tasmanian tiger hunt? I've learned a lot about endangered animals and ones that got extinct like quaggas. I'm especially interested in animals with stripes, too.

The executive secretary from the Town Hall was a judge in the pet show. He found out we were keeping a horse that's against the law and made us get rid of him, even though Loki was champion and won a year's feed. But he can stay with the rare animals at Wilmot Place while his food is paid for.

Jerry Brewster's father thinks that when Loki gets
popular with visitors, maybe the trustees will decide
to keep him and get a harness and cart donated for
him. Anyway, he's not common, which makes him
almost rare.

I miss having him here, but I can see him a lot,
because Jerry's father is going to run a nature study
day camp at Wilmot Place this summer, so Jerry and
I will be there most of the time.

My sister has a new kitten. Mom and Dad say I can
get a dog, even a big one, but I haven't yet. Loki
was the best present I ever had, and I will always love
him more than anything else. But since he can't
live here, the next best thing would be a Tasmanian
tiger cub. People, except for Jerry's father, will
probably think it's just a puppy with stripes.

I hope it's all right to ask. I was sure you'd want to
know about Loki and that I'm allowed to get a dog
now, and you might not guess without me telling you
that I'd rather have a Tasmanian tiger cub if there's
one to spare.

I forgot to say that Loki always runs to me when I
call him, even when I don't have marshmallows.

Love from
Matthew